EDITORIAL REVIEW

Thor's Dragon Rider
Book Five

Relinquished

"Norse mythology buffs will enjoy this compact installment in the Thor's Dragon Rider series." Virge B., Proofreader, Red Adept Editing

"In *Relinquished*, Kara, her fellow Valkyries, and Thor are on a mission to get a magical rope to bind Loki's son. On the way, they contend with a troll, irritable dwarves, and a squirrel who thrives on insults. Fans of the series will enjoy continuing to follow Kara on her journey." Susie D., Line Editor, Red Adept Editing

Hoodwinked

Relinquished

Shrouded

More To Come

Relinquished

Ebook first published in USA in June 2021 by Cosy Burrow Books

Ebook first published in Great Britain in June 2021 by Cosy Burrow Books

www.katrinacopebooks.com

Text Copyright © 2021 by Katrina Cope

Cover Design Copyright © art4artists.com.au

Published by Cosy Burrow Books

ISBN: 978-0-6450874-4-4

❀ Created with Vellum

*To the lounge chair adventurers - enjoy your newest
discovery into a high fantasy world.*

A bargain struck. A sacrifice made, and the price is high.

Loki's hound son grows stronger and his temper shorter, igniting fear in the gods of Asgard. They must restrain him before he becomes too strong to handle and brings Ragnarok upon them.

Desperate for a tougher restraint, Kara and Thor, accompanied by her trusty dragon and friends, travel to the realm of Svartalfheim, seeking the dwarves' expertise.

They soon learn that they will gain nothing without sacrifice.

Chapter One

Lightning forks just in front of Elan's nose, and thunder claps to the right, bringing a more ominous feel to the darkening sky. Zildryss jumps, releases Elan's horns, and scurries down her neck. Tiny talons pull at my black leather uniform as the miniature lilac dragon climbs me then circles around my shoulders. With wide eyes, he weaves within the security of my dragon-scale cloak before hooking his tail around my neck and peeking through the folds of the hood. Warm reptilian skin presses against my neck, warming it against the chilly air of the high altitude.

"That was close. Wasn't it, little guy?" My heart thumps forcefully against my ribcage, and I jump in my saddle when another lightning strike narrowly misses Elan's nose and forks beside the large golden dragon's left side, nearly hitting her flapping wings.

Zildryss's bug eyes briefly meet mine. In his usual

way, he doesn't respond other than to press closer to my neck, his small body warming as his adrenaline rises. I grip the reins of Elan's saddle tighter, pulling them closer together.

Elan's concerned eyes connect with mine as she glances over her shoulder. *I think Thor is getting a little bit carried away with himself.* Her voice speaks through my mind. *It probably wouldn't harm me. My scales should protect me, but I don't need you to get fried.*

Inching forward, I peer over the side between the gap of Elan's neck and her wing arch and spot Thor in his goat-pulled carriage. His legs are splayed, and his hammer is raised high. Lightning touches down on Mjollnir, highlighting the red in his hair, as his goats, Tanngrisnir and Tanngnjostr, weave through boulders and clusters of trees.

"I don't particularly want to be fried. Neither does Zildryss. His scales aren't as tough as yours. Your scales in this coat will protect us to some degree." I observe my exposed hand clasping the reins. "But there are still plenty of spots that could be hit."

Elan tucks her chin, watching Thor's progress. *What's his deal anyway? It's not like we're riding into war.*

"I don't know."

Looking over my shoulder, I spot Eir, Hildr, and

Britta on their dragons, Naga, Drogon, and Tanda. Each rider's face is pale, a stark contrast to the bright colors of the dragons. Even so, the scaly foreheads of the dragons are creased in frowns. Drogon's vast array of horns outshines his dull color. Several push together while he studies Thor intently.

Drogon's eyes meet mine, and his deep, grumbly voice penetrates my mind. *Somebody needs to do something about Thor. Our riders don't have dragon-scale cloaks like yours. This is putting them at risk.*

Another loud clap of thunder sounds just in front of Elan, and I jump. "Okay, Elan. That's it! Can you please take me down there?"

The sizeable golden dragon tucks her wings into her side. *I hope you're going to give that reckless god a tongue-lashing. If not, then I sure will.*

We dive quickly, careening toward the ground, narrowly avoiding any bolts of lightning. Elan's adjustments are quick, causing the arrows in the quiver on my back, tucked under my cloak, to play a dull tune as they smash against one another. Although I have complete trust in her ability, I surround us in a protective barrier, just in case she misjudges the sky-splitting electricity. When we reach several feet above the ground, Elan levels her body, dodging trees and hillsides and sometimes narrowly missing them as she follows Thor's progression.

I wave at Thor, but attempting to get his attention proves difficult because of his horned helmet clamped tight over his head, covering his ears. His prominent biceps bulge under his long sleeves as he shakes his hammer high above him. Thunder rumbles, and the darkness of the sky closes around us.

"Thor!" I call.

The god of thunder doesn't respond. His free hand smacks the reins down, encouraging the goats to quicken their pace.

"Thor!" I yell louder, only to be muffled by the hurried clopping of the goats' hooves on the stone followed by more menacing sounds of thunder.

Again, Thor doesn't respond, even after I scream his name at the top of my lungs. Despite the atmospheric noise, I'm surprised he can't hear me. We are barely above his carriage.

Here, let me. Swiftly, Elan clops Thor on the back of the head with her wing, knocking his helmet over his eyes.

Thor lurches forward, banging his hips against the front of the carriage momentarily, before jerking backward. The reins are still in his hand, and he accidentally yanks the goats into a sudden stop. He falls back, plunking to the floor of the carriage with a loud thud, and Mjollnir clatters alongside his helmet.

I chortle. "That's one way to do it."

Elan swoops in a circle and lands beside the carriage. Her talons click then scrape on the stone. *It was my pleasure.*

Thor glares at Elan. "Was that really necessary?"

Sure was. Nothing else was getting through to you. Elan straightens her neck, showing no signs of remorse.

Using the side of the carriage, Thor pulls himself up, collecting his helmet, then dusts his clothes. "So, why the urgent disruption?"

Remaining on Elan's back, I glower at Thor. "Do you think that lightning and thunder are necessary? I thought we were supposed to be coming in peace." I flail my arms. "You're acting as though we're here as an enemy, ready for war."

"We *are* coming in peace." Thor straightens the lumps in his leather jerkin by tugging at his hem then plops his helmet back on. "What makes you think we're not?"

Ah, all the thunder and lightning, Elan says sardonically.

Thor gives a deep chuckle and rubs his bushy beard. "I guess I got a little carried away."

Elan pushes back on her front legs, towering over

Thor. *Your getting carried away is putting all our friends in danger.*

Thor spots the three other dragons with their riders in the dark, clouded sky. "Oh. Sorry. I forgot. Oops!" He smirks.

Sliding off Elan's back, I push off the hood of my dragon-scale cloak, then I lean a hip against his carriage with my arms crossed. "You put the others and me at risk. Even though I've got this cloak, I can't guarantee it can protect me from your lightning. Besides, we're supposed to be coming in peace," I repeat as I approach the front of the carriage and scratch the goats behind their ears. "Why are you activating the thunder? It looks like we're about to start a war."

Thor shrugs, looking sheepish. "Sorry. I guess I'm a little apprehensive. The dwarves always put me on edge." He fiddles with the horn on his helmet. "I know they're only small, but they have magic, and they have deceived us in so many ways. It builds unrest and distrust."

I untwist a strap attached to one of the goats. "We want them to make us something that'll help restrain Fenrir. Remember? We need to act friendly, or they won't give us their help. Maybe we should slow down and remove the stressful edge from our search."

Thor's shoulders slump, and his chest caves with a loud sigh. "Argh. You're right." He grabs the goats' reins and brings them down with a light flick, and the goats' hooves clop casually on the stones.

I climb back onto Elan's back and pull the dragon-scale hood back over my head as we take to the sky.

Elan beats her wings steadily as she follows Thor's progress. *You know, I like Thor, right? He's not bad for a god and all, but he can be seriously dumb sometimes.*

I chuckle. "Don't hold back, Elan." With the absence of Thor's power, the dark clouds clear, exposing the bright blue of the sky. "He's not that stupid. He's just a little bit gung-ho at times."

That's one way of putting it, she says. *All brawn and no brains.* She chuckles.

"Elan!" I chastise. "I'm not criticizing Thor. He's the one god that has supported me ever since I started serving under him."

I'd have to agree with Elan, Drogon says. *He's often not the brightest star in the sky.*

"Oh, Drogon." I shake my head, appreciating the clear blue sky opening up ahead of me. Then I peer down the side of Elan's neck at Thor. His carriage is continuing along at a good, slow pace, his hammer resting on the bottom.

On my right, large trees sway, shaking their leaves violently. Shocked, I sit up straight. A monstrous form stomps through the trees, only several yards from the carriage and closing the gap to Thor. If it keeps up the pace, the enormous bald creature will collide with Thor's path within moments.

"What's that?" I ask.

Elan tilts her head toward the moving figure on the ground, and her wing strokes falter for a moment. *That there is a troll, and he appears as though he has his sights set on Thor.*

- Chapter Two -

The troll makes a destructive path toward Thor, leaving a trail of shaking leaves and branches in his wake. Thunderous footsteps rumble up to greet us, each one seemingly louder and more ominous. His figure is enormous, even from my place in the sky. Thor's bulky form almost appears to be the size of a large animal compared to the troll, who rushes forward, shoving trees aside with a mighty fling of his arms and rapidly closing the distance to the god of thunder. The giant pauses briefly to yank a tree from the ground. The roots grip the soil and give a brief final fight, desperate to cling to life. With a massive grunt, the troll charges and swings the tree. It smashes into Thor's stomach, sending him reeling out of his carriage and flying into a boulder several yards behind.

Dragon scales! They're as strong as the rumors

declare, Elan says. *They're also as big as the frost giants, if not bigger. I hope what they say is correct—that trolls are as dumb as hair on a dragon.*

The troll swings the tree in the opposite direction, releasing his grip and letting it fly over the tops of the other trees. It crashes to the ground hundreds of feet away. Birds and leaves mushroom into the air, and my jaw drops. I'm shocked by the distance. It takes me a couple of moments to yank my attention from the distraction and realize the troll is stomping his way toward Thor. My fearless leader lies stunned against the rock face, and his chin drops to his chest.

"Elan! We have to get down there and help him." My voice is almost a screech, and I lock my jaw to steel my emotions.

Without wasting a second, Elan tucks her wings and dives straight for the troll, then she stretches her wings at the last second. She drags her large talons along the troll's bare shoulders before twisting her body and whacking his back with her tail.

Lurching forward slightly, he arches his back and yells his frustration and agony at the sky. With his few brown teeth exposed, the troll slowly spins, searching for the cause of his sudden pain. By the time he faces our direction, I've covered myself with the dragon-scale cloak, and Elan has turned invisible, hiding every part of us. Little did I realize that Drogon, Naga, and Tanda had followed Elan. The troll screams as he swipes his massive arms at our friends, thinking they were the ones that caused him pain.

Naga maneuvers his smaller body out of the way and lands near Thor, with Eir clinging to his saddle straps. Without hesitation, Eir slides off Naga's back then darts to the thunder god to check his injuries.

The troll follows Naga's progress, and Elan quickly moves in front of the attacker. The reins tighten around my hands, and my body lurches sideways as she swivels, whacking the troll in the face with her tail. He blinks, and a frown creases his giant forehead. The troll's attention is finally pulled from Naga as Drogon flips and careens his horny head into the troll's back near the kidneys.

Struggling to dislodge Drogon's horns, the troll swings his arms back, mistakenly connecting with Tanda and Britta. The spinning motion dislodges Drogon's horns, leaving deep puncture wounds trickling with blood. Drogon flicks and twists as he attempts to gain control. Pale-faced, Hildr has white knuckles are white as she clings to Drogon's reins, stopping her from protecting them with her magic.

I ball my palms, twisting them in circular motions

around an invisible ball, before shooting the gathered magic as a protective barrier around Hildr and Drogon just in time to shield them from the trees and other obstacles in their way.

With fiery red eyes fixed on her friend flying uncontrollably, Tanda roars, then she expels a large plume of fire at the troll's stomach.

The troll clasps his stomach and gives a bellow of protest to the sky. "Quash just wants lightning to stop." Dejected, he slumps his shoulders, and he circles slowly, his arms drooping by his sides.

Eir pauses her observation of Thor to turn to the commotion.

Drogon regains control with a final flick of his body and instantly aims for the troll again.

Eir calls, "Naga, stop them!"

I stare at Eir in confusion. The troll, clearly named Quash, attacked Thor first, and we have to protect him and ourselves.

Quash digs in his toes, running straight for Drogon. Hildr stands in her stirrups, piercing the air with her high-pitched Valkyrie war cry. The troll continues charging toward them, swiping up a medium-size tree on his way.

Desperate to stop the troll from hurting my friends, I scream at Elan, "We have to help them!"

Without a second wasted, Elan swoops over the

troll's back, and another cry of pain leaves the troll. New, sizeable talon scratches line his back. The wounds are deep and weeping blood. He swings the tree behind him, narrowly missing Elan as she pumps her wings to take us higher. Shock fills his face when he doesn't find anyone behind him. I tighten my grasp to guard against Elan's sudden lurching movements. My white knuckles are clear to me, sticking out of the sleeves of my invisible cloak.

The troll screeches again, followed by a large groan. "Ahh! Quash just want lightning to go away. Quash doesn't like lightning. Now there are funny flying things surrounding Quash. They hurt Quash... and Quash not happy." A deep frown creases the troll's brow, and his shoulders slump once more. The dejected look is unmistakable as he scans the area then observes Thor. He pokes his thick finger in the dazed god's direction. "That man caused thunder and lightning. It scares Quash's family. Quash trying to stop him."

The troll steps toward Thor, and Tanda, Drogon, and Elan swoop down, circling the troll's head, ready to attack.

Naga's little voice calls, *Stop. Can't you see this troll doesn't want to hurt us? He's only upset by Thor's lightning and thunder.*

What are you talking about, Naga? Drogon grumbles. *This troll attacked Thor. We must protect our own. Surely even you as a peacekeeper understand that.*

The smaller blue dragon hovers just out of the troll's reach, partially blocking the other dragons' path. *Yes. I understand that. But he only attacked Thor because he wanted the lightning and thunder to stop. He was caring for his family.*

The troll swings his arms wide, dragging the medium-size tree through the air, and every dragon darts aside, narrowly dodging the tree.

Drogon's eyes narrow, and his deep, grumbling voice enters our heads. *It doesn't look like he wants peace.*

"I'd have to agree." Hildr lifts her nose and shifts in her saddle.

Suddenly, Zildryss ducks out from around my neck and flies down to the troll, circles him, then lands on the troll's nose before climbing to look at him in the eye. The tiny dragon's tongue lashes from one eye to the other, as he does when using his third eye. The lilac dragon's size is minuscule against the troll's nose and eyes. The troll wipes a finger on his nose, and Zildryss pushes off into the air, narrowly missing the hand. The little dragon flies lower and lands on the troll's upper lip, digging his little talons into the giant's skin.

The troll's eyes cross, and he gasps as though the

talons are tickling him. He sucks in a strong breath, accidentally sucking Zildryss up his nose.

I blink, trying to process the shock, and wonder what to do. In a split second, the little purple dragon has disappeared into the tremendous nasal cavity.

Chapter Three

The troll staggers backward, his face screwed in displeasure and his eyes narrowed to slits.

A high-pitched wail fills the uncomfortable silence. "Nooo!" Eir's face is pale as she stares at the troll's massive nose in disbelief.

What? That can't be. Did the giant really just— Elan stops midsentence.

"Suck up Zildryss?" I finish for her. "I think so." My mind is blank with confusion and shock, and I'm unsure how to act or help the poor little guy. I pull my hood back, hoping the fresh air will fill my mind with ideas, at the same time exposing my head and position to my friends.

Can we get him out? Naga's panicked voice fills our heads. *Is there a way?*

Each of the Valkyries' eyes lock together, searching for an answer.

My mind slowly churns over different options for

Zildryss's rescue, and I scratch my arm in frustration. "I don't know."

Drogon snorts out steam, his angry eyes fixed on the troll. *Ram him in the stomach. Maybe that'll get him to project the little guy out of his nasal cavity.*

Britta rubs her temple. "If he hasn't been sucked farther into the lungs."

With color slightly tainting her pale cheeks, Eir waves her hands, pulling my attention to her. "Can you use tickle magic?" She returns her hands to Thor's head, setting back to work on healing him, her eyes remain trained on me.

"Pfft." Hildr screws up her nose. "What kind of magic is that?"

A strange flash of irritation passes over Eir's face when she glances at Hildr. "Peaceful magic."

Hildr crosses her arms over her chest. "Trust you to think of peaceful magic to protect our friends on such a daunting creature."

Although I've seen peaceful magic work at unusual times, my brow creases with confusion. "Tickle magic." My voice betrays my apprehension.

"Yes. Tickle magic. Perhaps under the arms or something." She shrugs. "I don't know. My hands are busy looking after Thor. There's a split at the back of his head."

The troll's ugly face remains screwed with

discomfort, his vast eyes almost crossed as his body sways.

I scrunch my nose with uncertainty. "Okay. I will try. It's not something I've done before." Different scenarios spin through my head as I try to picture how I could tickle the enormous troll. My face screws in sympathy as I imagine what the troll must be feeling with the foreign object up his nasal cavity. Although I hold more substantial sympathy for Zildryss's predicament.

Narrowing my focus, I rub my hands together, picturing a perfect spot to tickle the troll.

Suddenly, before I have executed my move, the troll throws his head back and sucks in a large breath through his mouth then flings his head forward, expelling a massive sneeze. A small streak of purple shoots past us, flipping and twirling, with bits of ooze flying off with each turn.

"Zildryss!" I screech, grasping the reins.

Elan turns visible, swoops down, and lands over the little dragon. Drogon and Tanda flank her on all fours, ready to defend if needed.

I swing my leg over Elan's saddle, slide on my stomach down her side, and drop the distance to the ground. I dart under her large golden form to see the tiny lilac dragon splayed on the ground. Panic surges through me when I scoop up Zildryss. His eyes are closed, and his goop-covered little body lies limp in my hands.

"Zildryss! Are you okay?" After I turn him on his back, his wings flop down the sides of my hand, dripping snot to the ground. His lifelessness eats into my soul, and I long for the tiny dragon to show some fight. I run a finger, tingling with healing magic, over his abdomen. His chest rises and falls slightly, and I expel a sigh of relief. "That's it, little guy. Keep taking those breaths." Determined to help him along, I place my palm over his tummy and slowly release more healing magic into his tiny form. I don't want to deliver too much at once, in case it's too much for the little dragon.

Slowly, the rise and fall of his chest becomes more visible to my naked eye, and relief floods through me.

"That's a good sign," I whisper, rolling the tension out of my neck. "Just keep healing, little one." I continue to inject healing power into the tiny form and connect gazes with Hildr, Britta, then Eir.

Each Valkyrie nods in encouragement.

"It's looking good," I mutter just loud enough for them to hear.

A movement catches my eye, and I freeze. The troll stomps toward us, his large feet making the ground rattle. He swipes both his arms, which are as thick as tree trunks, at the two dragons that landed by Elan's side. Hildr's still on Drogon's back, and Britta has a white-knuckled grip on Tanda's reins, ready for impact. Both dragons narrowly dodge the swipe. When the troll's fists collide with the mountains, rocks clatter on both sides of Elan, and I shelter under her.

Elan's golden scales disappear from above me as she turns invisible, and the troll stomps toward me, his eyes focused on the little dragon. The warmth of a deep, trusting friendship engulfs me as Elan's hard scales nudge my back, and my dragon-scale cloak disappears from view. Confusion fills the troll's eyes, since the only thing he should be able to see is my head floating in midair. I drape my dragon-scale cloak over Zildryss and yank the hood over my head, turning us invisible. His stumpy forehead creases deeper over his oversized nose.

The ground rumbles as the troll stomps closer.

"Come on, little guy. You need to heal quickly," I beg, bracing my legs and ready to dive to the side. I push another wave of healing magic into his tiny form.

Zildryss's eyes fly open, and nimbly he flips the right way up, shakes off the excess goop. He then plunges over the side of my palm, glides to the ground, and stumbles toward the troll.

The blood runs from my face. He looks small and helpless. "Zildryss!" I cry. "Come back. Come back so we can leave."

Ignoring my calls, the tiny dragon charges toward Quash and halts within the space of one troll footstep. The lilac dragon stands on all fours, bracing his muscles, ready for action, and digs his talons into the ground. His tail arches over his back, and the point plunges into the earth, replicating a scorpion's strike. With eyes the size of dinner plates, the troll sinks into the rocky ground, buried up to his chest, with his arms secured by his sides.

"Huh! That's impressive!" Fascination covers Britta's face. She's still mounted on Tanda, to one side of Elan.

Despite the situation, I chuckle. "I forgot. Zildryss is spectacular with that magic. It's still hard to fathom that something so small can be so powerful."

Giving a smug yet humble look, Zildryss faces me, his tongue licking his eyes. After casting a glance at the troll, the lilac dragon makes his way to me. A large clump of goop slops from the top of his head and onto the ground. Wearing a look of displeasure, Zildryss pauses and shoots his wings out to the side, gives them one last shake, and flings off the remaining slime.

I chuckle despite the tiny dragon's predicament,

only to be rewarded with a warning look from Zildryss.

I raise my hands in defense. "I'll take you to a lake soon so that you can wash yourself off."

I catch golden scales in the corner of my eye when Elan turns visible, and although I didn't think it would be possible, the troll's eyes widen farther with shock over Elan's sudden appearance. He yanks his arms but is unable to remove his hands from the earth and expels loud groans of protest.

With Hildr still on his back, Drogon approaches the troll's side, and Tanda walks toward the other. Amusement plays on Britta's and Hildr's faces. They appear perplexed by how the troll had suddenly been buried two-thirds of the way into the ground.

After failing to free his arms, the troll swipes his body in a circular motion in an unsuccessful attempt to ward off the approaching Valkyries and dragons, filling the air with a frustrated cry.

Britta tilts her head to one side. "That's one way to stop him from attacking us." Her eyebrow cocks as she studies the little dragon, who is busy checking his body for the final remnants of the goop. "Has he done this before?"

Eir approaches from behind the troll, bracing Thor by her side. The thunder god's arm droops over her shoulders as he hobbles forward, his face still dazed in the only lingering evidence of his head wound.

The peaceful Valkyrie takes one look at the troll buried deep in the ground. "I'm guessing Zildryss has been busy. Although it's a magic Kara can do, it bears the work of Zildryss." Amusement lingers on her face. "It's a shame I missed it."

I nod. "True. Let's just say that Zildryss wasn't that impressed with being sucked into the troll's nostril and covered in snot."

The tiny lilac dragon rubs an open wing over some long blades of grass, wiping off the remainder of the goop. The disgusted expression on his face is almost comical.

"I think he had a score to settle." I eye the massive troll thrashing in front of us. "What are we supposed to do with him?"

Eir props Thor against a large tree. "Why, make peace, of course."

Hildr yanks her head back. "What?"

- Chapter Four -

Hildr slides off Drogon's back. Illuminated by the sun, her short, fiery-red hair stands on end, making her look angrier as she crosses her arms over her chest. Britta moves next to Hildr. Both Valkyries' eyes are fixed on the troll, and they shift farther away only when Quash's thrashing gets close.

Tentatively Naga advances toward them. *Eir is correct, you know. The troll was scared of the lightning and thunder. He must have been coming to protect his family and stop them from being scared. Naga thinks we should communicate with this troll to attempt to calm him.*

Drogon snorts, and steam shoots from his nose. He thumps his paws on the ground like a bull ready to charge. *Those are always your thoughts, Naga. You and Eir are always going for peace. This troll attacked Thor. Thor wasn't causing any harm. He was just getting excited over the pursuit of the dwarves.*

Naga straightens his back and spreads his pale-blue wings, exposing the white star markings underneath. *Naga knows Thor didn't mean any harm, but the troll did not. It made the troll scared, and now Thor's carriage and goats are gone.*

Hildr moves next to Thor, propping his arm over her shoulders. "Good point, Naga. Why don't you go and find the goats and Thor's carriage? The goats would probably follow you before any of the other dragons. While you're gone, we'll give your idea a go." Hildr takes on a large portion of Thor's weight, hoisting him off the trunk of the tree. "All right, Thor. Let's stand you in front of the troll."

Naga locks eyes with Eir, who nods. *I'll do that. But make sure you treat the troll nicely.* With one significant push, Naga takes to the sky.

Britta moves to the other side of Thor and props his other arm on her shoulders. "Let me help."

Comprehension starts to show in Thor's eyes, indicating his improvement and ability to think again. He aids the two Valkyries in taking him in front of Quash, and he tilts his head to stare up at the troll's much larger face.

Even buried mostly in the ground, the troll is still massive, and he towers over Thor. The troll's eyes narrow on the god. "You. You were the one causing that terrible sound and making the sky flash brightly."

Thor's bushy auburn eyebrows push together while he shakes his head, as though to remove the remainder of the fog in his brain. It only takes a moment before his eyebrows arch, and amusement flickers across his face. "Oh. Is that what your problem is? There was no harm in the lightning. I just got a bit carried away. That's all." He grins in an attempt to appear friendly.

The troll wriggles within his confines but has no luck loosening himself from the earth. His prominent, almost hairless eyebrows push together, forming a strange raised frown. "You scare Quash's family, and you scare Quash. Quash must make it stop."

"Whoa." Thor sways slightly as he lets go of Britta and Hildr and holds his hands in front of him, palms facing the troll. "Easy, my friend. Go easy. As I said, there was no harm intended. I wasn't planning on making any enemies in this realm."

I stand by Thor, my golden cape still draped over my shoulders. "It is how he says. Sometimes he just doesn't think."

With his eyebrows raised, Thor turns to me. "Now look who's accusing someone of not thinking."

"What do you mean?" I rock back on one leg to see my leader more clearly.

The god of thunder's light-blue eyes dance with amused accusation. "Well, by memory, I do believe you let Loki out."

Instantly, I'm on the defensive and cross my arms over my chest. "You know that was completely unintended."

A smug smirk curls up the edges of Thor's mouth. "Exactly. You acted without thinking of the consequences."

I huff. "This isn't about me. This is about your current actions and how you upset this troll, causing him to act out." Thor's comment got under my skin, and I can't help getting defensive. "You knew we were to come here in peace, not cause another war."

Thor grunts and raises his arms. For a moment, I wonder what he's doing, then his hammer flies through the air and lands straight in his palm and he closes his hand around the handle. "I come here with only peace intended."

Loud crumbling fills our ears, and we focus on the troll as he leans forward as far as he can, his neck bent to lower his face over us.

The troll's body casts the impression of a dark, menacing cloud. "Quash should eat you for dinner." He focuses on the hammer, and a breeze whooshes past us as the troll sucks a deep breath into his large nose. "You hold that terrible weapon again. It smells like dwarf magic."

"Ha." Thor swings his hammer in a circular motion. "Yes, it's dwarf magic." Stilling his hammer, he caresses the metal gently. "And I don't think eating us is the right thing to do. Threatening us so isn't going to make me put this hammer away. It certainly isn't a way to start a friendship."

An ominous darkness passes through the troll's eyes. "You holding that hammer sends a bad message to trolls. If you don't get rid of it and let Quash out, Quash will scream for his family."

Curiosity covers Thor's face. "Really?" He rubs his bushy red beard and pinches his chin. "Well, you, my friend, have just been buried three-quarters into the ground by a little dragon. I don't think you're very threatening."

The troll throws his head back and expels a loud groan of frustration.

Eir sticks her face between Britta and Thor, speaking over his shoulder. "I don't think that's helping, Thor. We're supposed to be making peace with Quash, not making him angrier."

Zildryss clings to Thor's tunic and circles his body, moving onto his shoulders and wiping his wings on the material.

"Hmm!" Thor tilts his head, observing the dragon and the trail of goop left behind. "Not what I had expected, little guy. I'm only letting you get away with that because you buried the troll and stopped him from attacking us." He rubs Zildryss's forehead with a playful roughness. "Don't expect me to let you do it again."

Ignoring Thor's reprimand, the lilac dragon circles the god's neck and settles down on his broad shoulders. His tongue lashes each eye as he observes the troll.

The troll focuses on the tiny dragon. "Quash didn't mean to attack your friends or suck you up. Quash was just wanting to protect his family. You seem like a nice dragon. Please, let Quash out."

Zildryss stares at the troll, appearing to be contemplating the idea.

Thor taps Zildryss's head lightly with a finger, causing the dragon's tiny head to bob up and down. "Don't you dare, little guy. First, we have to make sure he's not bluffing and that he's not going to attack us."

"Leaving Quash here will only make Quash more angry." The troll thrashes from side to side. "Let Quash out!" he screeches.

The ground beneath me starts to rumble. Dirt and rocks tumble away from the troll as his body rises from its depths. Quickly, I study the faces around me, searching for the culprit. Zildryss catches my eye. His eyes remain neutral, and he's still on Thor's shoulder, appearing not to be the one raising the troll. Every time I've seen him control the dirt, he has had his feet on the ground. Concluding that it isn't him, I move my gaze to Eir. She's the only other being I know in this group who can perform this magic. Her hands are raised, palms up, with her eyes focused on the area around the troll.

"Eir!" I scream. "What are you doing?"

Her eyes flick to me, and her concentration breaks. She drops her palms, and the ground halts its rumbling, fixing the troll within the earth, though his hands are barely buried beneath the dirt.

Eir flails her arms by her side. "I'm doing what we should do. I'm releasing him."

"What?" Thor barges past me to get to Eir, almost knocking me aside. He stops in front of her. "Why? He attacked us."

Eir balls her fists by her side and sets her jaw. It's the most defiant I've ever seen her. "He was only protecting himself and his family because he was scared." She raises her chin. "I'm not leaving him buried in the ground when he's done nothing wrong. We would've done the same. If someone scared our friends and family, we would attack."

"Here we go again." Hildr crosses her arms and leans on one leg. "Always the peace lover. Always seeing the good side in people." She waves a hand dismissively and turns to Britta. "It's the same argument over and over with Eir."

Britta nods. "Although this time, she has a point. The troll only did what she said, and it's exactly what we or anybody else would do if they thought they were being attacked. Maybe this time, there is a peaceful way to go about a resolution."

Hildr huffs, rocking her weight to the other hip away from Britta.

Thor stands tall, frowning down at Eir. "If you let him go, he'll just attack us again."

The defiant look remains on Eir's face. "I don't think so. Rather, I think if you stop conjuring the lightning and thunder, and we don't attack him, he'll go back to his family."

Thor expels a loud breath, and it hisses through his nostrils. He crosses his arms, the shaft of the hammer still in his grasp. "I'm not willing to take that risk. Besides, my carriage is still missing, thanks to him knocking me off."

"Quash just wants to go home." The large captive sticks out the biggest bottom lip I've ever seen. "Quash won't hurt anybody if you stop lightning and thunder." He aims his pout at Thor, and he attempts to pull out his hands but fails to release them.

The clattering of the carriage moves closer from behind us. Naga leads the way across the ground, with the goats' reins in his mouth.

"Thank you, sweet Naga. You're a gem." Thor smiles at the peaceful dragon then tosses his hammer and catches it again, turning his attention back to the troll. "And what if I don't believe you?"

"You must believe Quash. Quash tells the truth." The troll stops wriggling, his shoulders settling into a slump. "You are many. Quash is one. Perhaps Quash can do a favor for you. Then you let Quash free."

Amused interest crosses Thor's face. "And what do you think you can do for us?"

"Why are you here?" the troll asks. "Perhaps Quash can help."

Thor remains in a ready stance, even though the troll is appearing to be friendly. "We need a special binding created. One that looks like material yet is stronger than any chain on Asgard. We need the specialties of the dwarves."

"Ah. You need the sons of Ivaldi." The troll rubs his chin on his shoulder. "Quash don't know where they are, but Quash has a dwarf friend. Quash can take you to his friend Alvis. He hides from the daylight in a cave far not from here. The dwarves can't venture out during the daylight and must hide under the ground. Quash's friend might know these other dwarves you seek."

Eir spreads her arms, palms up. "See? He's even willing to help us. Besides, we do outnumber him, between the dragons and all of us, and we have magic. I think we need to raise him." She places a hand on her hip.

Pushing his bushy red eyebrows together, Thor crosses his arms over his broad, muscular chest and studies the troll. After a few moments, he exhales loudly through his teeth. "All right. Let's see if you'll keep your word. We need a little help in this realm anyway. I'm not familiar with where to find the dwarves."

- Chapter Five -

The ground rumbles and shakes underneath us. Rocks scatter and clatter against one another, and the dirt slowly falls away from the troll as he rises to ground level. Eir's dainty hands are raised, palms up as her magic pushes the troll upward. A look of pleasure fills the troll's face, yet his stubby forehead creases with confusion. After a few moments, the giant's feet are pushed to the surface and stop at ground level. He wears an expression that appears to be a mixture of bewilderment, shock, and appreciation for his newfound freedom as he sees his large, hairless legs freed from the earth's confinement.

"Okay, you great beast." Thor moves closer to the troll, tilting his head back to peer at the enormous creature's face. "Now it's your turn to fulfill your promise. Take me to this Alvis so that he may take us to the smith to create what we need."

"Quash is not a beast, but Quash will take you as promised. Follow Quash." The ground shakes slightly, and the leaves in the nearby trees rustling with each of the troll's footsteps.

Thor climbs into his carriage. After a quick slap of the reins, the goats spring into action, following the troll and weaving the smoothest path through the boulders and trees. The other dragon riders and I climb onto our dragons and take to the sky.

Gazing down at the rocky terrain, I'm amazed at how quickly the goats can weave the carriage from side to side. At times, I wonder how the wheels manage to stay on after being jarred from side to side.

The sun sinks over the horizon, casting long shadows among the trees, and the sky continues to darken, making it hard to keep watch. If it weren't for the troll's shiny head glimmering in the moonlight, it would be hard to follow. At least the dragons have night vision.

Kara. Elan's voice cuts through my thoughts as I try to follow Thor's progress.

"Yes, Elan." I wonder why she started the conversation like that.

I've tried, but I don't trust the trolls and dwarves. They may have good intentions, but I'm not certain. Dwarves live deep underground. The troll is probably leading us to one of these areas where I cannot go. We need to maintain communication.

I frown, not understanding where this conversation is going. "I thought you could always communicate with me if it's within a certain distance."

Yes, more than likely. But I don't know how deep you will go—possibly deeper than I can communicate. Even if I can still communicate with you, you can't communicate with me. You'd probably have to yell what you wanted to say, and I still wouldn't be able to hear you through all the rocks and dirt. Although my hearing is good, it's not as good as if it were mind to mind.

After a few quiet strokes of her wings, I ask, "What do you suggest?"

You have been practicing peaceful magic, have you not?

"Yes. You know I have. I just spent time in Alfheim to learn some, and you were with me. What does that have to do with anything?"

There must be some sort of magic that will help you communicate directly with me, like merging our minds.

I press my mouth to one side. "Hmm. I don't know."

I have an idea.

Sliding my hand under her scales just to the edge of the saddle, I take comfort in the warmth and hardness of her scales sandwiching my hand. "And what is that?"

Elan exhales, and her ribs cave inward momentarily. *Maybe that will help. You touch my soft flesh, and we'll give it a go.*

"What am I supposed to do? It's not something I've been taught."

Neither were you taught to ride a dragon, but we worked it out.

"True."

If you think about it properly, you'll be able to find the answer within you. I think it's deep within your veins. You've been practicing peaceful magic that helps you understand the elements. I'll open my mind and let you have access to it. It's up to you to push your thought into it.

I huff. "No pressure."

None at all. Humor marks her voice. *I think our connection is strong enough that we should be able to do this. You work on it, and I'll keep an eye on Thor and the troll. That way you can concentrate.*

Elan is right. It will be much safer if I can communicate with her through the mind. We could be in a lot of danger in our pursuit of dwarves, and undoubtedly we'll be separated from the dragons. The cool night air brushes over my face, pushing back my hood and blowing through my hair. I stick my hand deeper under Elan's scales, taking deep breaths to relax my body. Wanting an added connection, I shove my other hand under her scales as well and revel in the warmth of her tender flesh.

I close my eyes and become one with the rise and fall of Elan's body. The fresh oxygen stimulates my brain, helping me focus on the elements and opening my mind. Magic streams from my hands and into Elan's flesh as I will it to complete the circuit between our brains. When the current has been flowing for a few minutes, I send her my thoughts, willing her to hear them. *Elan. Can you hear me?*

Pride tickles along my magic. *Yes, I can hear you.*

She sounds slightly excited, and I push it away in case my success was a fluke.

That was quick. How did you do it?

Keeping my eyes closed and my exhilaration at bay, I center my focus. *I'm picturing my mind merging with yours.*

That's great! The wave of pride flows stronger through my newly formed bond, making the excitement harder to tame. *Although if you want to test it properly, you need to take your hands off my flesh and see if you can project your thoughts without touching me. Because when you're in the cave, you won't be able to have that direct physical connection, nor will you see me. Give it a go. Try with your eyes open and see if you can get past the distractions.*

Removing one hand from under her scales, I grasp the reins, then I remove the other hand. When I open my eyes, I focus on a fluffy white cloud floating not far in the distance then set to work connecting the circular stream between our minds. After repeating it several times, I add words to it. *Can you hear me now?* After waiting a couple of seconds, my impatience gets the better of me, and I ask again. *Can you hear my voice inside your head?*

Yes. I can hear you. Elan glances over her shoulder, her golden eyes shining with delight in the moonlight. *That was quick. Well done! I wish we'd had this advantage earlier. Then we could have held our own private conversations and left others guessing what we were talking about.*

Me too. But I don't know how you're going to keep me safe while I'm under the ground and you're out here, unable to get in.

Elan snorts out a puff of steam, sounding like an annoyed laugh. *You're right. I know I won't be able to be with you or get to you because of my size, and it's killing me. But I hope you'll be able to tell me where I can send someone to find you. Knowing that would kind of put me at ease.* Her worry travels down the bond. *I just hope you won't be too far away for us to communicate.*

Slipping my hand under her scales again, I reach for her soft flesh and hope that I'm sending her comfort through the connection. *I guess time will tell.*

We continue to fly in silence, the night sky closing the uncertainty around us like a cold blanket.

Elan's voice cuts through my thoughts. *It looks like we're here.*

Chapter Six

E lan circles and lands not far from the troll, whose head and arched, hairy back look more grotesque in the dim light of the night.

The troll stands at the front of a large cave that's too small for his enormous form to enter and yells, "Alvis! Alvis, are you in there?"

The only answer is the soft thuds of the other dragons as they land not far from Elan, accompanied by the rattle of the carriage rocked by Thor's impatient pacing.

The troll cups his hands around his mouth and calls again, "Alvis! Alvis, I have someone to meet you. Are you in there?"

Several moments pass before a gruff voice calls, "Yes, I'm in here. Why do you care?"

Elan's voice in my head cuts through their conversation. *I thought he said the dwarf was a friend.*

Yeah. I know, right. I agree. *Who needs enemies when you have friends like that?*

"It's Quash, Alvis." The troll doesn't seem put off by the dwarf's rudeness, and he continues his conversation through cupped hands. "I have someone that needs to meet you. He needs some help."

Alvis's attitude doesn't waver. "Why would I want to help anyone? You know better than to bring strangers here."

"This visitor is special," the troll continues. "And he's seeking help. You may want to take him up on this request."

"I don't take requests," the dwarf snaps, his voice echoing off the cave walls.

"Ah yes. Quash understands. Quash not stupid. But this request is from the god of thunder, Thor. He has asked for help to find the crafters."

Only the clattering of stone along the wall breaks the silence of the cave. The origin is a mystery, for it is too dark to see anything within the towering walls and ceiling cutting off the light from the moon. My eyes twitch awkwardly, lacking a point of focus as I stare into the blackness.

Elan's voice almost startles me. *He's coming.*

I squint, trying to find an outline of a small figure in the dark hole. *I can't see a thing.*

That's the benefit of dragon sight.

Ignoring the smirk in her voice, I snuggle my hand farther under her scales, embracing the warmth of her skin, and allow my magic to flow in a circular loop through her body then mine.

Oh. That feels strange. What are you doing? Elan wriggles slightly as though shivers are running down her spine.

Shh. I'm trying something new. I focus on the magic and send it to her eyes. My vision suddenly changes, and images have a dark yet clear distinction. The mouth of the cave and the troll are more transparent, and I can easily make out my friends surrounding me. Rocks clatter again deep within the cave, and Elan turns in that direction, taking my vision with her. A small two-legged creature, almost the shape of a tiny man, emerges from deep within the darkness.

Ha. I think I'm seeing through your eyes. I run my fingers softly over Elan's skin.

Really? That's fantastic!

The dwarf moves out of the darkness and raises a burning torch above his head, which makes his tiny form seem smaller yet accentuates his large head and nose. Pointy ears protrude from between his shoulder-length brown hair. As he staggers closer, his little body moves from side to side like it's a great effort for him to walk, his legs swinging wide with each step.

When the dwarf gets closer to the cave entrance, the light from the torch is enough, and I remove my hand from under Elan's scales. The dwarf's large, bushy eyebrows drop down into a frown then rise as he lifts his eyes to the dragon riders. "So, who wants to see me?" His eyes narrow as he takes in each creature before him, including the troll. "Who was rude enough to call me up from my cave?"

Thor clears his throat, and his boots catch a rock when he moves forward, making it clatter away. "I have requested to see you. We need to find the special smiths that work wonders with their art and magic."

He widens one eye, observing Thor. "And why would you want to see them?" The dwarf's gaze lands on Thor's hammer. "Looking at their handiwork lying within your palm, I guess you should already know who they are."

The god twists the giant hammer as though it's as light as a feather, observing the craftwork. He chortles. "Right. They did forge this, and I love it, which is why I'm here to ask for their help. We need special crafters to build a rope stronger than any chain on Asgard."

"And why would you need such a chain?" Alvis asks.

"We're attempting to stop the large hound, Fenrir, Loki's son. He has hit his teenage years, and his temper is escalating, making him more dangerous by the moment. Nothing is strong enough to hold him. We're afraid that if he's not bound, he will bring Ragnarok quicker than expected."

Alvis grunts, shrugging. "Why should I care? Ragnarok is a problem of Asgard's, not mine." He turns to leave, trudging a few steps away and not looking back.

Irritation flashes over Thor's face, but somehow he manages to keep it restrained. "As I'm sure you know, Ragnarok will affect all of the realms under the care of the Yggdrasil."

The dwarf halts and turns halfway back, crossing one arm over his tiny chest that's still enormous in comparison to his small body, and braces the inner elbow of the arm holding the torch. "I still don't believe you."

Thor's fingers tighten around the edges of his carriage. The shock on his face is illuminated by the burning torch. He seems not to know what to do next. Then his face hardens. "Then it will be your loss. It will be all of our losses if we do not contain this large hound."

The dwarf shrugs again but pauses halfway through turning to leave. "What will you offer me in return?"

Thor's body stiffens. "What do you mean?"

A wry smile creeps onto Alvis's face, and the shadows cast from the torch make his eyes seem evil. "Being a god of Asgard, you must have something I would like in exchange for my services. Do you think I work for free?"

"But it's for the good of the realms." Bemused, Thor rubs at his ear.

Grunting, Alvis tilts his head to one side then taps his mouth with an index finger and sucks in a whistling breath. "Like I said, you must have something that I want. A dwarf has needs. In fact, I'm in need of a bride. Have you got a daughter?"

I'm stounded when Thor's face brightens.

"Why, yes. I do have a daughter. Excellent idea. I even have a painting." Thor pulls a picture out of his side pocket and presents it to the dwarf.

Alvis snatches it from Thor and holds it up to the light of the flame. "She's a beauty. Clearly doesn't take after you."

Thor chuckles. "No. She takes after my wife."

I can't stay quiet any longer, and through clenched teeth, I ask, "Thor. What are you doing?"

Thor waves a dismissive hand at me. "Oh. Don't fret. That's why we have daughters. They are useful bargaining chips. What man doesn't want a pretty woman? Daughters are very convenient tools to arrange marriages to benefit us."

"What?" Hildr slides off Drogon, her hands balled into fists as she stomps toward Thor.

"Oh, relax." Thor waves a dismissive hand at her. "You're always a hothead, Hildr. It's a perfectly normal practice for the gods."

"Not at all!" Hildr's voice rises an octave. "How is it normal? She is a woman, not an object to be treated like a bargaining chip."

Thor shrugs. "That's what we do."

Expelling a loud groan, Hildr picks up a rock and throws it at the cave wall before stomping off.

Drogon watches Hildr's retreat. *I'm pretty sure you've just added an enemy to your list, Thor. Actually, make that two.* Drogon snorts out steam and follows Hildr.

Seeming undeterred, Thor watches Drogon follow his rider, the smirk on his face spreading. "What's their problem?"

"It's ludicrous." I slide off Elan's back, thinking maybe I can talk some sense into him. "Why would you trade a daughter?"

The sheepish look on the god's face widens. "That's just what we do. It's normal practice."

"For whom?" I swing my arms out to the side. "Does that mean that if I lose my purpose as your fighter, you'll sell me off as someone's wife?"

It takes all of my effort not to slap him when his smirk grows. "Well, if that's the way I find it best to proceed, for the good of Asgard, then that's how I'll proceed."

Exasperated, I groan, "Argh! This is ridiculous."

Somehow Thor appears genuinely perplexed. "I thought you wanted to get married."

I project all my anger and disappointment into a scowl and direct it at Thor before stomping after Hildr and Drogon.

Yep, you have definitely made some enemies, Thor. Elan says. *You might find Kara putting in for a transfer when she gets back.*

"It's just what you do." Confusion and innocence remain in Thor's voice.

The crunching of boots on stone catches my attention, and I peer over my shoulder to see Thor approaching the dwarf.

"So, new friend." Thor sounds like a salesperson ready to make a pitch. "What do you think? Do we have a trade?" He chuckles. "I hope so, as I've just made a couple of new enemies."

"Make that eight," Britta yells, tapping her foot on the hard rock floor.

Alvis takes another look at the photo. "I could sure do with a woman as pretty as that." The dwarf attempts to slap Thor on the back. Instead, the friendly pat ends up being closer to his backside.

Chapter Seven

The crunching of footsteps sounds behind me. Hildr, Drogon, and I move farther away from the cave, creating more distance between us and Thor. The god's idea of trading his daughter for information for Asgard has made me sick to the stomach. He isn't anything like I thought. I had hoped he was one of the better gods. Up until now, he has proven to be better, but now my blood boils when I think of what he is doing.

The stomping footsteps still follow us, and I can no longer ignore them. I turn to investigate and find Britta and Eir approaching us, followed closely by their dragons, Naga and Tanda.

Britta's scowl casts strange shadows on her face in the moonlight distorting her beauty. "I can't believe Thor is bargaining his daughter's hand in marriage."

Pulling on the straps, I adjust the weapons on my back. The clang of the arrows hitting against one another fills me with the urge to fire one and relieve some of this anger. I refrain, opting to hook my thumb in the leather strap instead. "I thought he was better than that. It sounds just like what some of the egotistical gods would do." I strike my palm against some dirt clinging to my leather uniform. "If Asgard's future weren't hanging in the balance, I'd turn around right now and go home."

"Wouldn't that put you into trouble with the gods?" Britta asks.

Moving to stand next to me, Hildr grunts, "Forget the consequences. I wouldn't stay here, either, if it weren't for Asgard."

I nod toward the cave's opening, which is encased in darkness, only the dull light of the torch illuminating the entrance. "What's going on over there?"

Britta glances over her shoulder then back at us. "Alvis has agreed to take us deep within the earth to the dwarves we seek. We have to travel through the tunnels, as nighttime is not very long here. The dwarves refuse to leave the caves during the daylight."

Standing up straight, I cross my arms. "Why not?"

"It's rumored that some of them turn to stone when the sunlight hits them," Eir says. "Because of this, they don't risk going into the daylight, just in case they're one of them. It's a horrible way to go, no matter how nice or terrible you are."

I screw up my nose.

Sympathy flicks over Hildr's face, and I wonder if I misread it in the moonlight. "That's not a nice way to live. I would miss the open air and sunshine."

"Yeah. It makes me feel sorry for them," Eir says.

Britta glances at the dragons. "So, we have a slight dilemma."

"What's that?" I ask.

"The dragons won't be able to come with us. They're not going to fit through all the caves and tunnels." She slowly rubs her black leather sleeve. "They'll have to wait here."

I connect eyes with my majestic golden dragon. "Elan warned me about this. I was hoping she was wrong."

When am I ever wrong? Elan snorts, and a light puff of steam washes over me.

I smile up at her. "I was hoping you were this time."

Tanda lowers her brilliant red eyes down to our level. *Make sure you take all of your weapons and charge up your magic.* Concern laces the once-menacing red eyes. Before she became our friend, her eyes always glowed with anger, but tonight they are etched with softness. *I want all of you to come out.* She sets her sights on Britta first then eyes each one of us individually. *Don't trust the dwarves.*

Britta runs a palm along the red dragon's cheek, and Tanda leans into it.

Drogon's brown head covered in horns is harder to see against all the rocks sneaking next to us as it lowers. *Don't trust anybody—especially someone who will trade his daughter for what he wants.*

Naga thinks Thor must have a special reason for doing this. Not that this makes Naga happy. Naga doesn't like beings being forced to do things, like we were once forced to be captives for the alliance.

Dragon snorts. *Always the one to think good of people.*

Compassion and tenderness shines across Eir's face as she strokes the underside of Naga's chin, and the blue dragon's eyes soften. "And that's why he's my dragon. Thankfully Asgard no longer holds dragons captive."

Naga leans in closer to Eir, nuzzling her hand.

Suddenly I'm nudged from behind. *Be careful, you.*

Turning, I find Elan's enormous nose behind me, and I spread my arms and hug her snout. *You know I'll be careful. You four look after each other.* I practice speaking from my mind to hers.

She blows a raspberry. *Like we need to be careful. We're four dragons together.* She nudges me again, and a cheekiness shines in her eyes. *Good to know you haven't forgotten your new gift already.*

I tap her playfully. *Of course I haven't forgotten.*

I glance around to see if any of our friends have noticed our silent conversation, but they are all too busy saying goodbye to their bonded ones.

Zildryss scrambles over Elan's head, flies down to my shoulders, and snuggles around my neck.

Good idea, Zildryss. You go with them, Elan says.

Britta pulls back from her goodbyes with Tanda. "We're going to have to leave the carriage here too. You dragons look after the goats. Okay?"

Tanda licks her lips. *I guess we can do that. Do they need to be alive when you come back?*

Britta looks wide-eyed at her dragon. "Tanda! Of course they do!"

Tanda smirks, showing off her large teeth in the moonlight. *I was joking. Or we could just make Thor walk. He deserves it after trading his daughter.*

"Don't tempt me," Britta says. "But no. Don't make the goats pay for Thor's stupidity."

Thor calls from the entrance of the cave, "Are you battle maidens ever coming?"

Just hearing his voice makes anger heat the back of my neck.

Hildr strides toward the cave, calling over her

shoulder, "Aww. The big, bad thunder god needs four Valkyries to protect him."

We chuckle and head toward the cave together. With one last glance over my shoulder at the dragons, we disappear into the cave and around the corner, leaving them standing by themselves in the open air.

As we trudge through the cave, our boots click on the rocks. Mustiness overtakes the fresh air the farther we progress. The tunnels weave and descend deeper into the earth. Alvis's torch shines brightly ahead but not enough to illuminate the rocks jutting from the cave's floor, especially with Thor's thick frame blocking most of the light. After the toes of my boots catch on rocks several times, I call to the flames of the torch, beckoning part of them to dance on my palm.

Hildr runs her palm over the flame flickering above my palm, her spiky red hair glowing in the light. "Is it warm?" She stops her palm over the tip before quickly jerking it back. "Ow!"

Britta chuckles. "Now, there's your answer."

Hildr's wide eyes are full of fascination as she gawks at the flame. "You'll have to teach us how to do that."

"It's easy." Eir holds her palm closer to Hildr. "All

you have to do is pull from your magic and picture a flame resting just above your palm."

Tilting her palm up, Hildr calls to the flame, her brow creased with concentration. The fire splits, then both portions hover above my palm. Slowly, one side starts to float toward her before snuffing out halfway through its travels.

Britta attempts the same from Eir's flame, and it slowly lowers, stopping a fraction of an inch above her palm. Pride sparkles in her eyes, only to dull when she sees Hildr's disappointment.

Witnessing Britta's success, Hildr tries again. After several frustrating attempts, Hildr slaps her palm on her black leather pants and groans with frustration. "I can't do it! How come Britta can do it so quickly?"

Eir places a hand on Hildr's arm. "Maybe because when you get stressed, you become too angry."

Hildr shrugs off her hand and grumbles, "Trust you to point out how angry I am."

Eir shrugs. "I was just trying to help."

Hildr's shoulders drop, and she lets out a gust of air. "I know. I'm just annoyed."

After quietly watching the commotion, Zildryss unhooks himself from around my shoulders. The chilly cave air tickles the warmth at the abandoned spot on my neck, and I shiver. The little lilac dragon launches from my shoulder to Hildr then shuffles around her neck before finally settling down, pressing against her skin above her fighting uniform's collar.

Hildr's footsteps falter, and her face turns blank as she stares at the dark void ahead of us.

I ask, "Are you okay?"

"Ha!" She exclaims, rushing to catch up with me, her cheeks flushed. "Yes. I believe I am."

She holds her palm up, focusing on the flame above my palm. It splits, then half of the flame floats toward her and stops above her palm. "Would you look at that? So that's how you do it." Her eyes are relaxed as she proudly gazes at her achievement. "Thanks, little guy." She strokes Zildryss's head and runs her finger down his spikey spine. "What an adorable little dragon."

- Chapter Eight -

With the flames dancing on our palms, we progress forward, following the strange dwarf and Thor. Alvis holds his torch low, and it exaggerates his size, filling the cave with his wavering shadow. His body sways from side to side, his knees stiff and refusing to bend.

Thor follows the dwarf closely, his towering form emphasizing Alvis's lack of height. Despite the cooler air in the cave, a layer of sweat builds between the god's shoulder blades, dampening a patch on his gray cape. It's as though he's nervous, and it sets me further on edge. I hope it's not because he senses a threat lurking in the darkness. Instead, I want his nervousness to be from him bargaining his daughter. I haven't met her, but I'm confident she doesn't deserve a life of being married to a man she doesn't love and forced to live underground in a foreign realm.

In the past, Thor has been a man of his word. Because of this, I held him in high regard. Trading off his daughter has dramatically diminished the respect I held for him.

Eir leads the Valkyries, with Britta taking up the rear behind Hildr and me. As the passageway gets narrower, the mustiness grows overbearing, and I long for a breath of fresh air. Still, I push forward, slowly becoming accustomed to the strange smell. When the passageway narrows further, I run my fingers over the hard, damp surface but remove them quickly when a chill crawls across my skin.

Zildryss circles Hildr's shoulder, his eyes wide and curious. Occasionally he jumps from Valkyrie to Valkyrie, even landing on Thor briefly as if to see the way. He wraps his tail around Thor's shoulders and peers over Alvis. The way the little dragon's body stiffens as he looks at the dwarf, I wonder if Alvis is Loki in disguise. It wouldn't be the first time Loki has tricked me by taking on another form. I study the dwarf's every move before my brain kicks in. Loki is locked up. Well, at least I hope he is. I can't place my complete confidence in the knowledge.

Suddenly, the ground shakes violently, and rocks ranging from small to the size of my head clatter from the stone ceiling and drop around us. Instantly, I douse my flame and shield my head with my hands. Simultaneously, I release a magic barrier, securing an arch above us and blocking the rocks. In my peripheral vision, I notice that the other Valkyries are doing the same. The darkness seems to make the shower much more threatening.

Zildryss squeaks, dives for Eir's neck, and circles it. The little dragon's panic stops him from settling and the whites of his eyes shine eerily in the torch's light.

Thor squats to the ground, shielding his head with his hands. I prepare to extend my shield to cover Thor when I spot Alvis's head barely visible over him. His face is calm, and he has his spare hand casually raised, creating a barrier over himself and Thor.

The dwarf slowly spins, his amusement over our panic clear. My blood boils as he chuckles. "Look at you lot. You can tell you're not from around here."

The cave shakes again then another time in short, violent bursts, bringing another shower of falling rocks gliding down our protective barriers.

Slowly the five of us rise to our feet. Despite the safety our magic brings us, we are still wide-eyed and on edge.

Thor stands, towering over all of us, and I drop one hand from holding the barrier and call to the flame in time to see the stress slowly leaving the god's face. "What was that?" Thor asks.

Alvis chuckles again. "Undoubtedly, Ratatoskr has just passed another insulting message to Nighogg from the eagle. It happens quite regularly in this realm."

Thor frowns at the dwarf. "But what has that got to do with the shaking?"

Alvis waves his torch as though it should be obvious. "Because the dragon is often offended. He gnaws at the roots of the Yggdrasil, attempting to knock the eagle off the top as a payback to the eagle's insults."

A bemused look crosses Thor's face. "I have heard about this, but I haven't experienced it to such a degree. And you say this happens frequently here?"

Alvis shrugs. "Yes, it's very common." He rubs his chin and gazes up at the tunnel ceiling, now still after the shower. "These walls are all secured by dwarven magic. Because it happens regularly, and we have to live in these caves, we have taken the additional measure for our safety. Only a few of the rocks that break away manage to sneak through."

Thor's gray cape billows as he places his fists on his hips and scowls. "A little warning would've been nice." His bushy eyebrows lower like a thundercloud.

"It didn't occur to me that you wouldn't be used to this. My apologies." However, Alvis doesn't sound the slightest bit apologetic. "Next time you come to visit, I'll make sure to let you know."

Thor glowers at the dwarf's retreating back before following him farther into the darkness, weaving deep underground.

After remembering I doused my flame, I beckon to the torchlight and transport the small fire to my hand.

Is everything okay in there? Elan's slightly high-pitched voice asks in my head.

I focus on pushing my voice through our bond. *Yes, Elan. Everything is okay.*

Are you sure? Elan doublechecks. *I just felt fear traveling across our bond.*

I'm certain. The cave had a slight rattle, and rocks fell all around us. It was frightening for a while, but we've been assured that it won't cave in on us. That's all you would've sensed. The drama is finished, and the threat is over, I say.

Elan's sigh of relief sounds through our bond. *Okay. That's good to know. You really did have me worried. I hate not being able to run in and rescue you. It's the only time I've been upset that my form is so big.*

I'm okay, Elan. Thank you. I smile despite myself. Facing the rock wall and running my fingers over the stone, I imagine I'm reaching closer to my dragon. The warmth in my heart for my friend pushes away the iciness of the rock.

"What are you smiling at?" Britta asks.

Quickly, I put on a straight face. "What do you mean?"

Britta moves closer, shining her palm flame closer to my face. "I saw your cheeks rise. I have no idea how you could be smiling after what happened." She waves a hand at the wall. "Plus you were stroking the wall with affection. That in itself is odd after what we just went through."

Playfully, I blow out her flame. "I was talking to Elan. She was worried. She felt my fear through our bond."

Britta splits my flame in two and beckons to one half. It floats over the small gap and dances an inch above her palm. "What do you mean, you were 'talking to Elan'?" She holds the flame up to my face again.

"I managed to learn how to speak to Elan through mind speak rather than saying the words. Elan made me practice on the way here. That way, I can speak to her if we need help or assistance or I need to give them a warning of some kind. You know they're all like mother hens, right? The dragons worry about us."

Britta nods.

"Elan wanted to hear me every step of the way."

Hildr frowns. "It's a good idea, but it's not like they can come and rescue us. We still in here on our own."

I tilt my head to one side. "I know. I guess she just wanted to keep up the communication so that she could understand every bit of worry she felt along the bond."

Eir's eyes glow in the dim light of the flame. "You have to teach us when we finish this trek. I would love to learn how to speak to Naga through my mind. It would be beneficial when we're parted or we simply don't want everyone to hear our conversation."

I smile at her enthusiasm. "I will."

The ground shakes slightly, grabbing our attention. Excluding Alvis, we all look up, checking the ceiling for falling rocks. To be sure, I erect my magical barrier, covering all of my companions, before we press on.

Thor casts me an appreciative look, ignoring my scowl. "How much farther?" he asks.

Alvis turns, and his torch casts shadows in the wrong places, making his appearance gaunt and creepy. "This cave travels extremely deep. How do you think we can hide our large population out of sight?" He raises an eyebrow, and the light eliminates the shadow for a moment. "You have no idea how big our population is, do you?"

Thor's shoulders stiffen, and he absentmindedly tightens his fingers around Mjollnir, a reaction I've learned is associated with insecurity. "I knew there were a few, but I didn't know how many. On the surface, during daylight hours, it appears no dwarves are living on Svartalfheim. I, however, know better than this because we have been taught otherwise." Thor scratches his wrist, still appearing nervous as we follow the dwarf into the darkness.

It's hard to push away the wrenching feeling in my gut as we move lower into the unknown, and taking in Thor's nervousness isn't helping to calm me. In order to drum up the courage to push forward, I focus on our mission. This trip is about more than us. It's about all of Asgard, including the nine realms that join the world tree. Fenrir is just one of Loki's children that are causing the threat, and now that Loki has been recaptured, the danger has grown.

"Aren't the dwarves friendly?" Even though Eir's voice is even, I can see her neck stiffening. She must've picked up on Thor's nervousness as well.

Alvis turns stiffly, and I'm swamped with the feeling of eeriness. "Whatever makes you think we're friendly? We're only friendly if it suits us. Most of us are quite hostile." He grins, and the torch illuminates his pointy brown teeth. A strange sensation churns through my stomach, and goose bumps rise on my arms.

Chapter Nine

I dart past Eir, grab Thor's upper arm, and yank him back. In the light from my flame, confusion shows in his blue eyes.

"You can't trade your daughter with this thing," I hiss in a low whisper, one eye on the dwarf's back as he continues to lead us through the dark tunnels.

Thor shakes off my hand and chuckles. "Battle maiden! You know I'm a man of my word. I always deliver what I promise." His voice is too loud for me to be comfortable, squashing my attempt to avoid the dwarf's attention.

Alvis pauses and peers stiffly over his shoulder. "What's going on?" He glowers at us.

Thor grins and makes a show of brushing each of his sleeves. "The young Valkyrie is attempting to stop me from doing something. But I am a man of my word, and I won't renege."

One of Alvis's eyebrows rises, and evil glints in

his eyes. "You'd better deliver what you have promised, especially your daughter. Or I could lead you to a spot you will never come out of."

Thor slaps the guide lightly on his back, making the dwarf lurch forward. "Do not fear, Alvis, my friend. I am a man of my word, and the Valkyrie knows it. I don't know why she's trying to convince me otherwise."

Thor casts me a threatening glare, and I hold my breath. The message to leave him alone on this subject is loud and clear.

Satisfied with my silence, he turns back to the dwarf. "Please, continue to show us where to find these dwarves to make our binding. I have many pressing matters to deal with in Asgard, and I wish to return as soon as possible." He nudges our wary host. "And the sooner I get back to Asgard, the sooner I can arrange for my daughter to come to be your bride. I assume this is what you want—my daughter, the sooner the better."

"Of course. I don't want to waste any time," Alvis snaps before leading us farther into the darkness. "And you'd better organize my marriage before you deal with Jormungandr. I don't care how much that serpent is thrashing and causing trouble."

Thor raises Mjollnir briefly, his knuckles white, but his voice remains steady and absent of any sarcasm. "Of course. Your marriage is much more important than any havoc Jormungandr is causing. It's like an everyday occurrence for the serpent."

My steps falter, and I stand rigid. I still can't believe Thor's determination to pass his daughter over to the deceptive being before us. He's even putting off his battle with the Midgard serpent and placing Midgard and other realms in more danger. I glare at the dwarf. Maybe he is Loki in disguise.

Britta puts her hands on my upper arms, gently guiding me forward. I take one hesitant step after another, weighed down by the turmoil inside that won't abate.

As the tunnel slopes deeper, it accentuates the eeriness of being stuck underground. It seems like we have traveled for hours, making me think the dwarf may be trying to trap us underground. We pass small lit rooms occupied by dwarven families, and the thought of raising a family here makes me cringe. There's no fresh air or water from a stream, only a musty, wet smell and water that tastes like minerals.

Each room we pass is filled with small families, their gazes unwavering as we pass by. Small flames burn on their sconces, yet the rooms remain mostly dark, making me think that perhaps the dwarves can see in the dark after generations of living underground.

Once the families seem confident we are here in peace, they get back to their chores. Each dwarf has their own shape, which to our eyes seems deformed in some way. Some have foreheads that are too large, some have enormous noses, and a couple of the women even have beards. Seeing beards on women takes some getting used to. I can't help wondering if the dwarves find this attractive.

Just when I start to get used to the dwarves' forms, we pass a room with much smaller dwarves, and I guess they must be dwarf children. By the chatter and activity, it appears to be a kindergarten of some sort.

Though I don't appreciate the dwarves' stares, each time we pass a room, it gives me hope that we're not being led to the depths of some abandoned cave to rot. Perhaps Alvis is leading us to the right place so that he'll be able to marry Thor's daughter.

After we pass a few more rooms, a dull ache builds in my legs. I'm surprised, since it is unusual for me to feel anything after walking. We have trained in the Valkyrie academy to be strong and fit, something I've maintained during my years of serving under Thor. Although I'm sure that we must have walked leagues by now. Or perhaps it seems longer because the trail is underground. There isn't much to look at, other than the odd room with a family here and there.

Eventually, clanging sounds through the tunnels, growing louder as we continue. The icy chill of the cave turns to wafts of warm air, the heat growing as we progress. It makes sense when we move into a large room. A forge burns in the center, and a couple of dwarf smiths work on either side, swinging large hammers and slamming them onto glowing red metal resting on top of an anvil.

The heat hits my face in a giant wave. I don't know how the smiths can handle the intense heat for such a long period. The closer we get, the more I can see the lines of sweat running down the backs of their tunics and gathering on their foreheads and chests.

The clanking grows louder, almost to the point that I need to cover my ears. It is a welcome relief when the smiths reach the stage of shaping more intricate details into the metal with chisels. The feeling of being ignored in a foreign realm is strange, yet this is precisely how the blacksmiths treat us, even when we are almost upon them. Each dwarf is building a different item. The dwarf on the left is crafting a sword almost longer than he is tall. The hilt is decorated with intricate carvings, and an emerald stone is embedded in the handle. On the right, the dwarf works on a golden pig that appears to be an ornament.

We stand in silence, waiting in vain for them to notice us. After a while, Alvis chuckles and says nervously, "These two talented dwarves are the sons of Ivaldi and are known throughout the land for their blacksmithing talents. They have fashioned many great pieces, including Gungnir, Odin's spear, and Skidbladnir, Freyr's ship."

Thor claps once, his face glowing with delight. "Oh yes. I am familiar with both of these. Fantastic works of art—not to mention the magic. Freyr lent me Skidbladnir not so long ago so that I could take it to Midgard and go fishing for the Midgard serpent."

The brothers continue with their work, seeming oblivious to our presence and praise bestowed upon them by Alvis.

Britta casts me a side glance and mouths, "Awkward."

I nod, flicking crazy eyes to the dwarves then back to Britta.

Eventually, the glow of the metal dims, and the dwarves lay their masterpieces and tools aside. With narrowed eyes, they finally look up, taking us in. The brother on the right nudges his glasses farther up his nose.

Thor straightens his shoulders as they scrutinize

him, and I find myself doing the same when they study the Valkyries before glaring at Alvis.

The brother on the left runs his hand over his few remaining strands of graying hair, which is long enough to cover only the slightest bit of baldness. "What is the meaning of this?"

Our guide bows, twirling his hand in an introductory motion before stretching it out to the side. "I'm Alvis, at your service. I have brought Thor, the god of thunder, and his entourage of wingless Valkyries. They wish to discuss something with you."

The two dwarves study Thor, observing Mjollnir and the belt wrapped around his waist.

The mostly bald dwarf glances at his brother before returning his gaze to Thor. "I see you have used Sindri and Brokkr. Why don't you seek them instead?"

Long, matted brown hair hangs down to the second dwarf's shoulders, appearing not only unbrushed but also bathed with sweat. "Yes. If their work serves you well, why would you change?" He peers over his spectacles, distaste curling his lip.

Thor inclines his head in a show of respect, yet a smirk turns up the edges of his mouth. He steels his emotions before returning his gaze to the dwarves and places a hand over his heart. "I'm afraid that though you know who I am, I am at a loss as to your names."

The unwashed dwarf grunts. "And that is the way we prefer it. Now, answer the question."

Thor inclines his head again. "Fair enough. Yes. Sindri and Brokkr have served me well. I am especially grateful for their work, but your work also precedes you, even though your names are not publicly known. I believe it's your talent that we require."

The dwarf with long brown hair taps a finger on his pressed lips. "And what would that be?" He hitches his pants, exposing his round belly for a second, before glancing briefly at the golden pig he was creating, as though to check it is still there.

Thor clears his throat. "You may be aware that the monster children of Loki and Angrboda are causing trouble among the realms."

The dwarf on the left leans forward and scowls. "When aren't they causing trouble?"

Thor nods, his red, shoulder-length hair swaying and shining in the glow of the fire. "True. They have been known to cause trouble in the past, especially Jormungandr. But this time is different. Fenrir has grown, and with his increased strength, he has become hostile, especially since his father was captured."

The dwarf on the right huffs and crosses his arms. "You know all our services come with a cost."

Thor rests his hammer on its head beside his leg. Stones scratch under its heavy weight. "And your services are worth the cost. However, in this case, it's for the good of all the realms. We need to work together to rid the realms of this threat."

The dwarf with the matted brown hair wrinkles his nose. "I'm not sure that we're feeling that giving." As though to confirm his statement, he glances at his partner.

A frown forms on the brother's forehead, and a breeze blows his sparse strands of hair into his eyes. He combs it over his scalp with his fingers. "Tell us what you need, and we will think about it."

Chapter Ten

Thor gazes at the two dwarves, dumbfounded. It appears he's not sure how to continue his argument. A moment passes before he takes a visible deep breath. "As I mentioned briefly earlier, we have the problem with Fenrir. The hound is getting too big and strong. His temperamental personality is escalating, and he is becoming a threat to many beings. He blames us for locking up his father. I'm sure you're aware that Loki is a mischievous god, and his recent mischief has been against Asgard's interest and safety."

The dwarf on the right tugs at a scorched spot on his sleeve. "Of course we know about Loki. His behavior is often unwelcome in Svartalfheim."

Thor scuffs the stone floor with the toe of his boot. "Yes. Because we have secured him, his son, Fenrir, is becoming quite aggressive, and his size and strength are proving a problem. The gods have restrained the hound in chains many times, all to no avail. He has managed to break out of every one, including ones that we have welded ourselves and took several gods to carry and loop around his neck. Only once did it take Fenrir a moment more to break out of the chains."

Thor paces the room a couple of times then pauses, facing the dwarves again. "This instills a deep fear in the gods, and rumors are stirring about the escalation of Ragnarok and the downfall of Asgard. If this happens, it will also bring the downfall of the realms connected to the world tree." Thor spreads his arms wide in a humble gesture. "Which means Svartalfheim as well, in case you are unaware."

The brother on the right lifts his glasses to the top of his head and snaps, "Of course we know this will also affect our realm. We may live within a rock most of the time, but we're not stupid and closed off from the rest of the world attached to the Yggdrasil." When he scowls up at Thor, his glasses topple off the back of his head. Turning swiftly, he catches them before they smash on the rock floor. "It's rather insulting that you should think otherwise."

Thor raises his palms and wobbles his head. "I

was only checking. I cannot assume what you do and do not know. I apologize if I offended you."

After placing his glasses on, the dwarf gruffly waves his hand dismissively. "Oh. I was only messing with you. But I still don't see why we have to do all the work to protect the realms."

Thor purses his lips while rubbing his beard. "I was hoping you would see it more as protecting yourselves and your loved ones. And everyone else in the realms just happens to be lucky enough to benefit from that."

The balding brother rubs the muscles on his right upper arm and connects eyes with his brother. "I guess we can look at it that way. What do you need from us?"

Thor taps his hammer several times against his calf excitedly. "Do you have something strong enough that would secure the hound?"

Tapping his chin with his finger, the dwarf with the thinning hair says, "I think we have just what you need. But we will need some ingredients. They are unusual, and it may take a while to find them."

Agitation flashes across Thor's face. "What are they? Maybe we can help find them."

The dark-haired dwarf laughs, deep and heartfelt. "I doubt it. When we say the ingredients are unusual, I mean it. They are the stomping of cats and the beards of women." He chuckles. "Okay, not that hard from some of the dwarf women." He continues to rattle them off, counting on his fingers. "The roots of mountains, the spit of birds, the breath of fish, and the sinew of a bear." He glances over at his brother. "Am I right?"

He nods. "Yes. That's right, Shorty."

A strangled noise comes from Thor. Deep lines of amusement crease the edges of his eyes.

"What?" the bald dwarf asks.

Thor clears his throat, and the smile drops from his face. "Forgive me. From my height, your calling your brother Shorty tickles my amusement."

The dwarf plants his fists on his hips. "Well, he is short. He's a whole inch shorter than me, so that's his nickname. My nickname is Tallie. He got the hair, and I got the height."

"Oh. All right. That makes sense." His eyes travel from one dwarf to the other as though he's trying to spot the difference. "Of course. I can see it now." Although his tone indicates his uncertainty.

Tallie huffs. "I'm glad you see it." He strokes his chin. "Now, where were we?"

"You were talking about finding the ingredients," Eir prompts him.

"Ah. Yes." Tallie lifts a finger. "I'm sure *we* will need to find the ingredients. I don't think these useless Valkyries and the god of thunder would even know where to start in our realm."

The spectacled dwarf nods. "I suppose you're right." He gazes at the Valkyries and Thor. "It will take some time. You'll need to entertain yourselves for a while. Perhaps Alvis can show you around the realm." He says it as though our guide doesn't have an option. "We need you out of our way so we can concentrate on our work. If we're distracted, we will make more mistakes, and it will take longer. If you need this completed soon, then I'm certain you'll understand. Alvis seems willing to please. I'm sure he can keep an eye on you."

"Oh, I understand,." Thor says. "We don't have any intentions of stopping you from working." He raises a bushy eyebrow at Alvis. "I'm sure Alvis will be happy to show us around and entertain us while you work. I trust that we'll be entertained well under his guidance and care."

Alvis crosses his arms over his chest and taps his tiny boot on the rock floor. "What's in it for me?"

The god of thunder grabs his hammer off the ground. "I believe the reward already discussed is large enough." He spins and tosses Mjollnir then catches it again.

The displeasure of not receiving additional compensation for guiding us further flashes briefly across Alvis's face. "I suppose it is. I guess if it helps the sons of Ivaldi speed up the process, then it would help me get my bride quicker." He faces the two dwarves. "How long do you need?"

"At least a full day," the dirty-haired brother answers.

"Oh." Alvis grumbles. "So long?" He tosses his head to the side in disappointment before he eyes us. His shoulders sag. "Okay, then. I'll show you around." He waddles toward a different exit from the one we came through, calling unenthusiastically over his shoulder, "What would you like to see?"

Thor peers at us. "I know I would like to smell some fresh air again. How about you, battle maidens?"

Hildr groans. "Oh yes. I'd love to smell some fresh air."

Alvis frowns then snaps, "We can't go out in the daylight."

"I don't care," Hildr says. "As long as it's fresh air."

Alvis redirects to a different exit not far from the first. "Fresh air is coming up, then. I would have thought that you would want to see more of our fantastic lifestyle. Not to worry." He waddles through the exit, grasping both sides of the stone tunnel and pulling himself up the first ledge.

Without being asked, we fall into place, keen to get out of these caves. We weave through the tight corridors, passing more family caves branching off.

I brace myself against the narrowing space, only to have my hands slip. After grabbing some of Alvis's torch flame, I investigate the cause. A small stream passes through some cracks. It trickles down the side of the wall and follows a groove carved into the lower wall. I hold the flame closer. The crevice looks man-made as though chiseled into a river, providing them with natural water from a lake.

The path veers slowly upward, passing several more families interacting in different rooms. Each time, we are met with stares filled with mixed emotions, some hostile and some merely curious. They mustn't get many nondwarf visitors down here.

My legs ache again, making me think we must have traveled miles, but I'm unsure. Being trapped underground has messed with my senses. Either way, the time seems to drag on forever, adding to the emotional drain of dealing with potential enemies around every corner.

Thirst torments my throat, and I scoop up some water that dribbles down the walls in a thin river and suck it into my mouth. My nose crinkles. The over-powering taste of minerals, probably collected from the river's path over the rocks, is bitter on my tongue. I stick it out in disgust. "How much farther until we get to the top? I would love a drink of fresh water."

Alvis's annoyed sigh bounces off the tunnel walls. "We're not even halfway there yet. Have patience."

Chapter Eleven

Kara! Elan's voice startles me in the darkness of the tunnel.

I hold a hand over my heart. *What's wrong?*

How much longer are you guys going to be?

I run a hand over the moist stone wall, using it as a guide while focusing on speaking through my mind. *Quite a while, I think. Apparently it's going to take about a day. Why?*

I'm starving, Elan complains. *We could fly off and catch something, but we don't want to catch the wrong thing and cause more trouble in this realm.* She groans. *And you should see the drool coming out of Drogon's mouth when he stares at the goats attached to Thor's carriage. It's almost hilarious, except they do look rather delicious.*

A hand grasps my forearm, and I'm met by Britta's keenness. "Are you talking to your dragon again?"

"It's that obvious?"

She nods. "Yeah. You get this funny look on your face, like you're concentrating extremely hard. What's she saying? Are they doing all right?"

I huff a laugh. "Elan is whining about being hungry, and apparently Drogon is drooling over the goats—literally."

Thor glances over his shoulder. "They have food in front of them. What are they complaining about?"

Annoyance flicks through Britta's eyes as she peers at him. "The only food in front of them are the goats."

A strange expression crosses Thor's face. It almost looks as though he thinks we're stupid. I hold my tongue. Maybe my anger with him over trading off his daughter is tainting my perception of him.

He doesn't respond, probably because he already knows he's treading on eggshells.

"What's that look for?" Hildr snaps, her scowl deepening as her eyes narrow on him.

Thor shrugs. "Well, the goats can be eaten," he says matter-of-factly.

"Aww!" Eir moans. "The poor goats!"

Hildr fists her palm, snuffing out the dancing flame. "Then what will pull your carriage? You're not using our dragons." Her arms fold over her chest.

Thor ignores her hostility and chuckles, and a

slight smugness laces his voice. "I thought you knew that the goats can be eaten."

"Of course," Hildr snaps. "I heard you the first time. We realize goats can be eaten. But I think you're missing the point. Then they'll be dead, and you won't be able to pull your carriage."

"Tanngrisnir and Tanngnjostr are different from normal goats. They are special. I wasn't trying to be demeaning. I thought you knew." Thor sounds genuinely perplexed. "If the bones aren't damaged, as in they don't break and the marrow is intact, the goats will be re-formed in the morning. They will come back to life as adult goats."

"That's ludicrous." Britta's voice echoes off the stone walls. "As if any animal would submit to a life of that. The poor things would be tortured every single time."

Thor shakes his head. "Not if it's quick. I've eaten them a few times."

"What?" Eir's face pales.

Thor looks sheepish. "I know you're all animal lovers. I am too. But I've been to a few places where I find myself starving, with nothing else to eat. It's advantageous when I've traveled far and am about to go into battle. They are always resurrected in the morning. Simple. It's part of the magic associated with Mjollnir. Kara, tell Elan that the dragons can eat the goats. I realize they're not as big as cows, and they have to share, but make sure they don't damage the bones so that they can rise again in the morning. The dragons don't have to starve."

The light cast from Alvis's torch retreats farther down the tunnel, leaving ominous blackness behind Thor's back.

I gaze at him in disbelief for a while longer then yield. After all, they are goats, and everyone who eats meat consumes some sort of animal. I'm not close enough to drum up a magic food source for them. I sigh. "I guess I can tell them. I should have thought ahead and left them some magic food. I didn't realize we would be gone this long. If they don't eat, the dragons will be rather irritable when we come back."

They all watch me, and I push them out of my mind along with the diminishing sounds of Alvis's footsteps. He's not waiting for us. I focus on talking to Elan.

The cheer I get when I relay the message of the goats is loud and clear, and I don't want to hang around to listen to Elan's pleasure as the dragons devour them. I'm sure it'll make me sick to the stomach.

Zildryss curls around my neck, as though sensing my discomfort, and I scratch him behind his two big horns on the back of his head. The goats' fate to repeatedly become food makes my stomach churn.

We return to our trek through the tunnel, and I run my fingers along the chilly, damp walls as we attempt to catch up to Alvis. The air warms slightly and carries a freshness my lungs long for as we spot the back of the dwarf, his head glowing under the torchlight.

The ground shakes violently, and this time my feet lift briefly off the floor. My knees buckle, and I collapse to the ground, a rock jabbing into my thigh. I groan then raise my hands to assemble a protective barrier above all of us, then I notice Eir has beaten me to it, just in time to stop a rock from falling on my head.

"Is Nidhogg chewing on the roots of the Yggdrasil seriously causing all this destruction?" Britta asks.

Alvis turns, acting as though we were never left behind. "Of course. What else would it be?"

"We don't have such an adverse reaction on Asgard." Thor wipes his brow with his forearm and rises to his feet. "I'm glad too."

I groan. "I would like to get my hands on that little squirrel. He has caused so much pain because of his insults and mischief."

Amusement flashes over Alvis's face. "I shall take

you to the tree, then. That's no hassle at all. Then you can call him and tell him what you think." He progresses forward then pauses and calls over his shoulder, "Although you'll have to have an insult to pass on to someone to get his attention."

I scowl at the back of Thor's head. "Trust me. That's not going to be a problem." Despite my enthusiasm, my mouth feels dry. "But first, I would like a drink. Is there a lake nearby?"

"Coming right up." The dwarf paces a few hundred yards farther.

Fresh air wafts onto my face, and I sniff, sucking in its beauty while raising the flame on my palm, searching for the roof of the cave. My flame fails to illuminate it.

"We're almost there," Alvis calls.

"We are not," Hildr says, her hasty footsteps clacking on the stone to catch up with us.

"Can't you see there aren't rocks above you? Hold your flames up in your palms and have a good look," he snaps and swings his arms, the flames spluttering their protest as his torch arches above him.

A wave of disappointment rushes over me. "I've already tried that."

We spread out, searching for the edges of the cave, but find nothing. Another breeze caresses my face, and I take a long, deep breath, overjoyed that I can smell the fresh air. I lower my flame below my waist. Tiny twinkling lights sparkle in the blackness above. "I can't find the cave walls, but I can see stars." My knees buckle slightly. I almost kiss the ground and hug a tree. I'm so happy to be out of those caves. "Please take us to the lake. Then I'd like to go to the world tree and summon that rat."

"Don't you mean the squirrel, Ratatoskr?" Hildr asks.

I don't hide my displeasure. "It's the same thing."

Chapter Twelve

"Well, here it is." The dwarf's face shines in the moonlight recently unveiled from a large cloud. In the semidarkness, I barely recognize the trunk of the Yggdrasil. Leaves rustle in the breeze, playing their soft tune above our heads. The dwarf grunts as though he's just performed a great service for us. "You call to Ratatoskr now. I hope you have that insult prepared. If you don't, it'll be amusing to see you become the brunt of his insults."

Alvis moves away from the tree, and I approach it, placing my palm against the trunk. I call up the tree as I did in Midgard. "Ratatoskr!" After a few moments of silence, I call again. "Ratatoskr!"

Leaves rustle loudly in a sudden gust, and their shadow passes over us like a sweeping wave. The clouds have cleared completely, exposing the full brightness of the moon. I stare into the branches, searching for any sign of red fur. I think I spot a hole farther up the trunk. It sits under a constant shadow, making it hard to define.

"Ratatoskr!" I call again, ignoring the awkwardness of calling to an empty space. At least I'm mostly surrounded by friends who are familiar with Ratatoskr's ways. "Where are you, Ratatoskr?" I raise my voice. "Ratatoskr!"

"My friend." Thor's voice interrupts my thoughts. I turn to see him talking to Alvis. "I would love to see a little more of this intriguing realm while Kara speaks to the messenger. Could you show me around?"

"Why would you like to see more? It's dark. There's not much to see," Alvis says, grumbling.

"Under the moonlight, I'll be able to see plenty. I'd like to see more of the land my daughter will be moving to."

"In that case, I guess I can show you what a spectacular realm this is," Alvis says eagerly. The clacking of rocks scattering across the ground announces their departure.

A few moments of silence pass while I wait for some sign that the messenger heard me. I probably don't have to yell, for I won't be surprised if he has magical hearing, enabling him to hear all the beings calling him, ready to send an insult to someone. But besides the leaves playing their tune, it's silent.

I call again, allowing my pent-up annoyance to seep through my voice. "Ratatoskr!"

"He must be close by now." Eir's long, light-brown hair sways in the breeze as she gazes up into the branches. "He can move quite quickly when he wants to. I've seen him talk to people soon after they have called." Locks of hair fall across her face, and she gathers the strands, weaving them into a braid before securing it with a band she yanks from her wrist. A couple of wisps fly loose on either side of her face.

My neck aches from gazing up, and I give the search a rest. I lean my upper arm against the rough bark of the trunk and cross my ankles. "He's certainly taking a while this time. I'll give it a little longer."

Something careens from above and hits me on the forehead. It's tiny, but my skin stings. It hit too hard to have simply fallen, and my suspicion rises, leading me to believe it was thrown. When I can't see anything, I call to Britta's flame and pull it onto my palm before lifting it, checking for a glint of red fur. Something flies at me again, this time smacking my cheek. The sting is instant. "Ow!" I rub my cheek. "That's going to leave a mark."

"Good! That's to remind you to be more patient next time. I'm a busy messenger."

I hold my flame up higher, stretching on my tiptoes, and catch a glimpse of red. It circles the trunk downward then pauses on a branch not far from me.

"You didn't have to throw things at me," I protest, still rubbing my cheek.

The rodent tosses a paw in my direction. "You are rather daft. I have to remind you somehow not to be so impatient." He balls his paws into fists and places them on his hips, straightening his back and standing tall. His beady black eyes, peering over his long nose, seem condescending. "Now, do you have a message for me to carry or not? Remember, it—"

"It has to carry an insult." I interrupt him and roll my eyes.

Ratatoskr puffs out his chest, showing off the patch of white fur on his underbelly. "Exactly."

"Then you need to come down here so I can pass on the message without yelling it." I indicate a branch in line with my head.

Reluctantly, Ratatoskr climbs down the trunk and perches on a branch a few yards up, arms crossed.

I hold back my annoyance but narrow my eyes. "I need you to carry a message to Thor."

He raises a bushy eyebrow. "The word is that you are traveling with Thor. Why can't you give it to him yourself?"

Eyes downcast, I reply, "Because even after everything I've done for him, he doesn't seem to take me seriously."

"Huh. I wouldn't take you seriously either." Ratatoskr climbs farther down the trunk but still makes sure that he remains higher than me. "So, what's the message?" He lifts his pointy nose and sniffs the air.

"Pass this message on to Thor." Ridding my palm of the flame, I place my fists on my hips. "Thor, I'm extremely disappointed in you. I thought you were going to be better than all the other gods of Asgard. Instead, I found out you are as low as them, if not lower. You pretend to be an honest, caring being, yet you're willing to trade away your daughter instead of choosing one of the several other ways available to get what we need. I'm appalled and disgusted, and I no longer want to serve under you."

"Ha. You're finally learning something." Ratatoskr polishes his claws against his white chest fur. "What you say is no surprise. I knew the god of thunder wasn't any better than the other gods of Asgard. I'm shocked it took you this long to realize it. You're a slow learner, aren't you?"

"Say what you will, Ratatoskr." I want to tell the squirrel about how Thor stood by me when I was exiled from Asgard, unlike Ratatoskr, who took pride in telling me the news. Yet it's hard for me to compliment my leader because of what he's willing to do to his daughter. Instead, I tap my foot repeatedly and glower at the rodent. "Can you please stop getting Nidhogg angry? It's leading him to chew the roots of Yggdrasil, and every time, he causes Svartalfheim to shake violently. I wouldn't be surprised if other realms attached to the world tree are being shaken also. It's dangerous."

Ratatoskr shrugs, and I want to shake the smirk off his face. He leans against the trunk and crosses his ankles. "That dragon can do whatever he wants. I'm just the messenger carrying the eagle's message down to the dragon. It's not my fault he takes it personally and takes his frustration out on Yggdrasil's roots. After all these years, you'd think he would've learned."

"Isn't it destroying the tree?" Eir shifts beside me, her peaceful face strangely distorted with annoyance. "If the tree is killed, it'll destroy all nine realms. We won't even need Ragnarok."

"Maybe that's the plan." Ratatoskr scurries down the trunk and into the distance, possibly to find Thor.

Hildr barges past me, knocking my shoulder as she watches the disappearing rodent. "What?" When she realizes the rodent has covered too much ground to catch up with him, she faces us. "Did that idiot just say what I thought he said?"

"I'm afraid he did," Britta replies, standing next to her. "That squirrel is worse than I thought. Not only does he bring insulting messages to many beings, he also sounds pleased that it's causing some kind of destruction for the nine realms."

"What a rascal!" Hildr snaps, hitting her fists on her hips. "I mean, I knew he was a warped little rodent, but that's just atrocious."

We wait by Yggdrasil for Ratatoskr's return after he passes his message to Thor. Time ticks along, and I wonder how far Thor has traveled with Alvis. It's taking the fast-moving squirrel much longer than I anticipated. Every moving shadow captures our attention. Uncertainty of what may approach us in the realm places each of us on guard.

Crunching footsteps sound behind us, and we turn to find Thor stomping toward us from the opposite direction. His face is a mixture of amusement and bewilderment.

When he's within a comfortable hearing distance, I ask, "Did Ratatoskr find you?"

His face is strangely blank, and it takes a few moments for the question to register.

"Oh, yes. Thanks for the lovely message." I think there's a flicker of amusement in his eyes.

My brow pinches into a frown. "Wasn't it insulting?"

"Of course it was." He chuckles, leaving me bewildered. "Your insults are getting better." The amusement leaves his face, and his eyes look haunted.

Britta slowly turns clockwise, searching. "Where's Alvis? You didn't kill him, did you?"

Thor tosses his head back, his eyes wide. "What?" I think I see guilt flash over his face. "Oh no. I didn't kill him. He certainly didn't die by my hand." The shake of his head seems a little too insistent.

"Okay," I say hesitantly. "Then where is the weird dwarf?"

Thor rubs the back of his head under his thick auburn hair. "I sent him an insult through Ratatoskr. I had the messenger take him away to speak to him and word the insult so that the dwarf wouldn't know that it came from me."

"Then I guess they'll be back here soon," Eir says.

The look on Thor's face is strange. "Maybe." He leans against the trunk, pressing his hands between his backside and the bark of the Yggdrasil.

Strange, I think, secretly eyeing him. Something is weird about the way he's acting.

Chapter Thirteen

D eep lines crease Thor's forehead as he stands pressed against Yggdrasil's trunk. Every few moments, he tosses Mjollnir, flipping it for a few rounds before resting against the trunk again. He appears to be deep in concentration, with an expression that rarely visits the god of thunder's features.

"What's gotten into you?" Hildr's voice, as harsh as always, cuts through the silence.

Thor's frown deepens, and he tosses the hammer for another round. "What makes you think there's something wrong?"

"For a start, you've been standing there for a while, just tossing that hammer and looking deep in thought. It almost looks like you're pining. Are you having second thoughts about bargaining your daughter away?" Her mouth twitches, and she doesn't bother hiding her spite as she leans on one leg.

Ignoring Hildr's remark, Thor looks off into the distance, where a tiny sliver of sunlight pierces the dark sky, his thoughts seemingly far away.

"What? Don't you have a comeback?" Hildr presses. "You certainly look like someone with a guilty conscience."

Eir groans and murmurs, "Just leave it, Hildr. If he's having second thoughts, he doesn't need you harping in his ear. Let him think it through. Perhaps he is thinking that. Perhaps not. I don't know." She turns to Thor and lifts her voice. "Are you sure Alvis hasn't ditched us here and gone somewhere else?"

Thor doesn't say anything but continues to stare at the horizon. The slit of sun grows, spreading glimmering light.

I ask, "What exactly did you get Ratatoskr to say to Alvis?"

Strangely, my leader ignores me.

I press further. "Are you worried that he's abandoned us to defend against the dwarves alone?"

Thor huffs.

Finally, a reaction.

"Worried? I don't think so." He nods in our direction. "I have you four with me, and I have myself and my trusty hammer." He raises Mjollnir, and his biceps bulge through his long sleeve. "I'm sure we could find a way back to the dragons and the carriage one way or another. The goats should have resurrected by now."

His gaze travels across the horizon another time, the light hitting the whites of his eyes. "If Alvis doesn't turn up shortly, then we should leave anyway. We don't know if he's a dwarf that will turn into stone when hit by the sunlight. It may have even happened." Thor shrugs. "I don't know if this turning-into-stone-in-the-daylight business is true, but I'm not waiting around all day for him to come back." He rests against Yggdrasil again, crosses his ankles, and resumes tossing his hammer.

We leave him alone to his thoughts and wait impatiently for the dwarf.

Seeing the sunlight again relaxes my muscles. I didn't realize how much I missed its light shining across the lands and the fresh air that accompanies it. It's also comforting that we can see the land and any threat that may come with it clearly. I'm not looking forward to returning to the caves' darkness and stale air. I can't fathom how the dwarves can dwell in the stagnant atmosphere, hidden underground for most of their lives. It must be depressing. Sunlight usually brightens any mood.

Eir rubs her upper arm, appearing worried. "How are the dragons doing?"

"I don't know. I haven't talked to Elan for a while."

A frown creases her forehead.

I continue, in an attempt to place her at ease, "I'll see if I can reach her from here."

Concern passes through her eyes. "Ask about the goats. I want to make sure they're alive again after being devoured by the dragons."

Across the bond, I call to Elan, pushing out my thoughts, as she taught me during our flight here. *Elan.* When she doesn't respond immediately, I call again, *Elan.*

Oh. Elan's muffled yawn sounds through the bond. *I'm just waking up. How's everything?*

So far, uneventful. How about you? Are all the dragons okay?

Huh? Okay? Of course we're okay. We're dragons.

I smile. Usually, she would be right. *You never know. There are some enormous monsters out there.*

You don't have to remind me. We've tackled a few of them together. Not something I'd like to relive. She yawns again. *We had a small meal of the goats last night. Half a goat doesn't go very far for a dragon, but it was enough to quench the hunger.*

That's great! Have the goats come back to life, like Thor said they would?

Yes, they're here bleating away and telling us off. Well,

I guess that's what they're doing. I don't speak goat. She pauses, and I can feel a tinge of tension traveling across our bond. *It's actually not pleasant.*

They probably remember what you did.

Elan's shiver travels down our bond. *Ew!*

I don't know. I'm just guessing. I can't imagine much worse, so give them some slack. It's good that they're okay. Thor says that being emergency food is their morbid gift. The thought leaves me unsettled, and I attempt to change the subject. *I'm glad you're all okay. I just wanted to check in.*

Warmth travels down our bond. *Thanks for the update. Stay safe.*

You too.

After scurrying over the other Valkyries' shoulders, Zildryss jumps onto my head. His talons catch in my hair as he runs in a circle.

"Ow!" I slap the top of my head to press the pain, narrowly missing him. "What are you doing, Zildryss?"

I wait for him to show me through visions. Instead, he lurches from my head, flaps, then lands on Eir's head before progressing to Hildr's. Finally, he leaps forward and flaps his wings until he lands on Britta's brown hair, his talons messing up her tight ponytail. His purple feather-like wings flail, and it appears as though he is indicating something.

I follow his motioning, and my gaze lands on a speck of red in the distance, slowly making its way through the bushes. I have to stare at it for a while before I realize who the dejected, red-furred form is. He slowly stumbles forward, his shoulders slumped and his feet dragging, leaving lines in the dirt.

"Ratatoskr?" I ask hesitantly, uncertain that my vision isn't betraying me. I'm shocked. I've never seen him move so slowly. It almost looks as though he's upset over something, which I didn't think was possible.

The second I mutter the squirrel's name, Zildryss holds still, halting the ruckus on Britta's head. The tiny dragon flies from Britta to Hildr's shoulder before landing on Eir's shoulder, his tongue licking each eye. His small mouth has dropped open and widens farther for a moment before he shuts it and continues to lick his eyes while staring at Ratatoskr.

"Aww! He looks dreadful!" Eir empathizes with him.

I place my fists on my hips. "Yeah. For the first time, I actually feel sorry for him." I watch him take step after slow step, dragging his feet and slumping his shoulders.

Thor pushes off the world tree and turns around to find out what we're looking at. I can't see his face, but his shoulders stiffen. There is no sign of Alvis or any other dwarf, and I wonder if the dwarf has done something terrible to the squirrel. Not that the squirrel didn't have it coming, but it's so strange to see him this way.

When Ratatoskr finally comes within a few yards of us, he raises his drooping little face and points at Thor. His chin quivers. "You." His claw shakes. "You. What did you make me do?"

Chapter Fourteen

The squirrel's claw wobbles all over the place as he points at Thor. It takes me a moment to process the wreck that stands before us. It's so strange. Never have I seen Ratatoskr like this. He has always been snarky and rude. I still struggle to believe this is Ratatoskr.

His wide stunned eyes narrow as he stares at the god of thunder, his voice husky as he repeats himself. "You. Yooou! What did you make me do?"

An indifferent expression rests on Thor's face as he raises his palms and shrugs. "I don't know what you mean." His tone is steady, although I think I hear a slight wavering of uncertainty at the end.

With his red furry legs wobbling, Ratatoskr shuffles closer to Thor, each step firmer than the last. "That place you made me take him to tell him your insult. It was too far away. So far that we couldn't get back to the cave before daylight. I took him out there, and I gave him your message. Then…" His jaw quivers again, and his eyes glaze over. "Just like that, the sunlight shone over the thin trees, breaking through their leaves. We searched for a nearby cave or large tree trunk, but there were none. Daylight in all its glory hit the dwarf. He turned to stone in an instant." The little bottom lip quivers again. "Stone. Stone, I tell you."

Thor wipes his brow with his forearm. "I don't know why you think I'm involved. I didn't make him stay out in the daylight. There must've been enough cover for him under the trees or something. Surely."

"I told you. The trees were spindly and the mountains far. Nowhere could he hide from the killing light of the day. He's out there." The squirrel points his little trembling claw in the direction he appeared from. "He's out there, frozen in stone midstride." He repeats as though Thor needs some help understanding the severity.

My jaw drops, and the other Valkyries and I look at one another's surprised faces before turning in unison to Thor. *Did Thor just plot to have Alvis killed so that he didn't have to give away his daughter?* Part of me rejoices because this means he didn't want to trade his daughter's life by forcing her hand in marriage. But the other part is horrified. It's not the first time that the god of thunder has killed enemies. Still, this seems more like a betrayal.

Avoiding our gazes, Thor pulls at the hem of his tunic, yanking it straight. "I don't know how you can point the finger at me." Anger grows in his voice. "I didn't make him stay out in the daylight. I'm sure he knew more about his condition and the possibilities than me. I had no idea whether he was one of the ones that would turn to stone. I had heard rumors, but I didn't know if they were true, and I certainly didn't know it would affect Alvis." He flails his arms at the messenger. "And besides, I'm sure you knew about that rumor. If you cared about the dwarf as much as you make out, then you wouldn't have kept him out there."

It takes a moment for Ratatoskr to respond. He holds his mouth agape as he stares at Thor as though slapped. Then the squirrel suddenly narrows his eyes, pulls back his shoulders, and dusts off his fur with the back of a paw. He then rakes his claws through the white fur on his chest and down his stomach. His shoulders shimmy as though he's shaking something off, then he lifts his gaze, his eyes harsh black beads, the way I'm used to seeing them. "I don't care for anyone. How would you think that? I'm a messenger. I simply pass on messages, and the more insulting they are the better." With that,

Ratatoskr darts up the world tree trunk and disappears down the hole.

We stare at the hole in shock. It's an effort to pull my thoughts away from the hole and mull over the situation to try to figure out whether Thor was trying to kill the dwarf.

Thor peels his eyes away from the hole and takes a deep breath. His shoulders droop, and his gaze falls to the ground. He doesn't seem to notice that I'm watching him. He squares his shoulders. "Right. We should keep going. Clearly, we're on our own anyway." He bends to pick up his hammer, which he discarded when Ratatoskr pointed an accusing claw at him.

Hildr fiddles with her hair, running her fingers through the auburn spikes, her attention zeroes on Thor. "So, did you do it?"

"Did I do what, Hildr?" Thor asks, exhaustion betraying the resignation on his face and squashing the strength he gathered moments earlier.

"Did you get Ratatoskr to kill Alvis so that you wouldn't have to hand over your daughter?" Strangely, a hint of compassion shines through Hildr's direct questioning.

"Ratatoskr didn't kill Alvis. The daylight did," Thor corrected her.

"You know what I'm getting at."

"If you're asking whether I arranged it…"

Hildr nods.

He scratches his bushy beard. "I didn't know how long the night would last here or how far away the sunlight was." He tugs at the edge of his tunic's sleeve. "Did I want to give away my daughter's hand in marriage to that scoundrel? The answer is definitely no. It was all an act. And I understand each one of you being upset by it, but I had to play the part." His gaze lands on me, seeking compassion. "I hoped you would be the one to believe me, Kara."

Guilt constricts my throat as I look into his deep-blue eyes, and I swallow, struggling to remove the lump. I should've had more faith in him. I should've known from how he's treated me over the past couple of years that it's not like him to do something like that. Instead, I doubted him, and for that, I will be forever in his debt.

He has stood by me at the worst of times, even when I accidentally let Loki loose. He stood up to his father and defended my honor in the eyes of Asgard.

With a heart heavy with remorse, I mumble, "I'm sorry" and cast my gaze to the ground. "I should've known better."

Footsteps crunching on gravel approach, and a large hand rests on my shoulder, strangely bringing me comfort.

"I understand. I would have questioned me too."

I search for the malice in his voice and blink when I find none, sweeping away the welling tears. "But I still should've known you better than that." I raise my eyes to meet his and become caught up in their compassion. The guilt oozes out of me. I don't know how he can forgive me so quickly.

He wraps an arm around my shoulders and directs me to face the others. "Come. Let's go. We need to get back to the sons of Ivaldi. Hopefully they have finished the restraint."

Zildryss flies to his shoulders and settles after completing his usual circling ritual. The lilac of the little dragon is a strange contrast to the god of thunder's red hair.

I grab my weapons pack and sling my sword between my back and my quiver then fall into step behind my leader. My shoulders tense as we enter the caves once more. The musty air and the confinement send my muscles into overdrive. I fix my eyes on Thor's back, and Zildryss seems to be playing hide-and-seek with me from underneath Thor's hair. Despite my apprehension about returning to the caves, I grin at the tiny lilac face every time it appears. Each time he licks his eyes, my spirits lift, and I'm pulled from my deep thoughts, breaking the tension of the ominous silence. At times, I even chuckle, the sound echoing off the stone walls of the corridor.

The tiny dragon gives his antics a rest after my third outburst of laughter, and he once again snuggles up to Thor's neck, hiding under his hair.

The echoes change. Instead of my giggles, the scuffing of boots and the crunching of stones follow us. We pass a room, and once again the dwarves' stares follow us. Some don't look so friendly at seeing other beings in their home. This time, we don't have Alvis leading us to dampen the shock of our presence. When we pass one of the rooms, the stares are so hostile that I jump when Zildryss lands unexpectedly on my shoulder. When he rubs himself around my neck, it takes away the majority of the discomfort.

The corridor darkens once again, and I realize I haven't made my own light source. I stop and execute the magic to carry the flame on my palm, pinching it from Britta as Eir moves in front of me, following Thor. With my fire dancing on my palm, I fall into step behind Eir. Somehow the slight space added between Thor and me emphasizes the distance I added to our friendship. Even though Thor says he has forgiven me, a chill enters my heart. I should have supported him.

As though sensing my distress, Zildryss snuggles

his warm body against my neck, hooks his tail around the back, and climbs down to my chest. He stares up at me, his tongue dashing from eye to eye. The warmth he sends into my neck somehow finds its way down to my heart, pulling me from the depths of sadness. I'm glad this little dragon decided to join us. Suddenly an image shoots into my head. It's of Thor and me communing together with trust and friendship, still working by each other's side for the good of Asgard. Warmth cocoons my heart.

Chapter Fifteen

Finally, we reach the end of the path after a long and tense trek to the furnace room. Thor pauses just out of sight of the room a couple of feet into the tunnel, and he smiles over his shoulder at me. At first, I'm rooted to the spot, unsure, and I blink a couple of times before I smile back. A weight lifts off my shoulders. We've taken a step toward confirming the image Zildryss showed me earlier. I still don't know if Alvis's death was in Thor's plans, but I'm glad he is no longer giving his daughter away as a bargaining tool. In any case, I never liked the dwarf, and in many ways, I'm glad he isn't in our lives any longer. Something about him made me not want to trust him. It wasn't just his appearance, and now I know he wasn't Loki, as my mind entertained briefly. The dwarf's natural appearance was unusual compared to the shape of the Valkyries and the Vanir and Asir gods, but it wasn't what made him untrustworthy. Something about Alvis sent shivers down my spine.

We approach the middle of the furnace room. The sons of Ivaldi labor intensely over a piece of fabric so thin that it's hard to see from this distance. Their backs arch over a spinning wheel that whirs rapidly while their feet and fingers work nimbly. The thread stretches between two different wheels and needles.

"How is that going to restrain Fenrir?" Britta whispers over my shoulder. "It looks almost as thin as the fabric of a dress that females wear to a ball. Or worse still, as thin as a spider's web."

Shorty flicks his matted brown hair away from his face and peers over his glasses at her. "Looks can be deceiving." His eyes travel between us. "Where's the dwarf that brought you? I don't see him among you."

We Valkyries stand in silence, and Thor inches forward. "No. He has not returned. We don't know where he is. We assumed he abandoned us when we were on the surface. I was under the impression that he believed he had completed his duty to us." Not even I can see the telltale sign of a lie on the god's straight face.

Tallie looks up from his work with an eyebrow cocked. "So you decided to make your way down here by yourselves?"

The god spreads his arms wide and squeezes his lips together. "Yes. We simply followed the path back." He approaches the dwarves to peer at their work and is shot down with a warning look. He pauses his approach. "How are you coming along with the restraint?" He is moving the conversation away from Alvis, but the dwarves don't seem to notice.

Shorty holds the rope up to the light and pulls it taut. Light shines through the fabric, making it seem flimsy and weak. "It doesn't look like much, but we guarantee this magic weave is stronger than any chain you can create on Asgard." He runs the rope over his hands, letting it slide through his stubby fingers. Pride fills his features. "You've returned early, but that's all right. We were just placing the final touches on it."

"Fantastic!" Thor claps once. "Then we will wait in the corner and let you finish what you're doing. I would hate to disturb you. Thank you, kind sirs." He bows slightly at the dwarves, showing them respect for their work.

The dwarves peer over their noses and incline their heads slightly before setting about finishing their work. The sword and the pig they were working on when we arrived sit unfinished to the side, waiting for the dwarves' attention. Only the whirring of the wheels fills the room as we make our way to the corner.

We sit quietly, watching them at work. Zildryss moves along the Valkyries then settles on Britta's shoulder and curls around her neck. Peacefully, his head rests on his front talons, and his ribs rise and fall with each steady breath. My heart melts. He's an adorable dragon, full of talent yet so humble. I'm glad he showed me the image of Thor and me getting along in the future. I was worried after I betrayed my leader's trust and doubted his true intentions over giving away his daughter.

As though reading my thoughts, Thor smiles at me then sits on the rocky ground with his knees pulled to his chest and rests his folded arms on top. "You know, I think my daughter, Thrud, would like you Valkyries. In fact, I wouldn't be surprised if she wanted to join the Valkyries." His voice ripples with amusement. "If she knew that I had tried to give away her hand in marriage, I think she would kill me." He huffs, shaking his head in disbelief. "To be honest, I think she'd be scarier than you four believing I was going to trade her off."

"Sounds like someone I'd like to meet." Hildr stretches her legs, the leather of her black uniform groaning in protest. "I'm gathering she doesn't have wings."

Thor chuckles. "No. She doesn't have wings."

Britta sits forward. "Then she will definitely fit in with us wingless Valkyries."

"Although I think she'll fit in with *all* the Valkyries." Eir brushes a wisp of long hair off her face. "The winged Valkyries no longer treat us like servants, remember? I know it used to be different, but we must learn to forget what they did to us during our early days. It was in their training. They didn't know any better."

"Oh, Eir. I don't know how you do it. You always see the good side of people." Although she gets straight to the point, as always, for a change, Hildr's tone isn't condescending.

Eir's eyes shine brighter. "How do you think I remain friends with you?"

Britta, Thor, and I chuckle, each attempting to keep it quiet so as not to disturb the dwarves.

Hildr scowls. "Nice. Have a laugh at my expense."

I rest a hand on her shoulder. "Hildr, you are a loyal friend with a good heart, but you can be quite abrupt at times."

After only a moment, Hildr's laugh joins in with the chorus. She reaches over us and nudges Eir with her fist. Eir joins the laughter.

"Ahem." Our chuckles are interrupted.

We gaze up to find both of the dwarves standing not far away holding the flimsy rope in their hands. It's quite long, if not longer, than some of the longest chains that have been used on Fenrir. Stretched between the two, the fabric appears extraordinarily light and flimsy. In unison, they hold out their cupped hands, and the rope swings from their palms, trailing to the floor on either side of them. The fabric is thin and almost white, again making me think of a spider's web.

"We are done." Shorty holds it toward Thor. "Your rope is ready to restrain the hound. It should hold better than any of your chains."

Thor scrambles to a squatting position, his head still higher than the dwarves'. He runs his hands over the drooping material, squeezing the fabric between his fingertips. "It's incredibly thin. Are you sure this is going to be as strong as the chains?"

"Stronger. That is part of the beauty," Shorty confirms.

Thor stands. The light from the sconce on the wall illuminates the dwarves' faces as they stare up at his full height.

"Thank you very much. You have served the nine realms well. I will make sure that the word that you made this is spread."

The brother with the thinning hair lifts his chin.

"We will be proud to have our work credited to us. We stand by our craft."

The brothers roll the fabric into a tight bundle and hand it to Thor.

"May the nine realms be safe," Tallie says as he combs his thinning hair over the top of his head with his hand.

Thor bows respectfully. "Thank you again. Now we will be on our way."

Chapter Sixteen

E ir grabs a bag from inside her weapons pack and hands it to Thor. "Here. Put it in this."

"Thank you." After bundling the rope neatly, Thor slings the backpack over his shoulders. "Let's get out of here."

We all nod, wasting no time to enter the tunnel to head back to the dragons.

As I move into the confinement of the tunnel, the walls seem to close in around me. "I can't wait to get some fresh air and get out of this dank cave." I motion to a sconce on the wall and steal some of its flame, calling it to my palm. It's nice not to have to well my magic for some time before being able to use it. This is one of the things that makes me grateful for my time spent in Alfheim.

The other three Valkyries grab some light from the sconces for their palms, illuminating the path ahead that lacks wall lights. Eir leads the way, then

Thor, with me treading in his footsteps and the other two following close behind. Even with our lights, the tunnels are still too dark and damp for my liking.

The ground shakes, rattling stones from the ceiling. Once again, I erect my barrier, protecting us from the falling rocks. "Ratatoskr must be back at work, passing on the eagle's insulting messages to Nidhogg."

Britta crouches behind me. "I can't wait to get out of here. I hate the ground shaking like this, especially when we're trapped in the caves." Voice quavering, she continues, "It's putting a great deal of faith in magic, hoping it will hold the ceiling. It's not like it's a little shake." When the shower of rocks stops, she lowers her hand, which she used to help me extend the barrier, and we continue.

Longing for our realms' still ground fills me. "I'm glad Asgard is farther away from the roots of the tree. It must shake all the way to the top for the eagle to get the message, but the tremors seem worse in this realm."

We pass another entrance to a nook built like a home. "I can't wait to be rid of all these dwarves staring at us every time we pass," Britta whispers behind me. "I know we're passing their homes, but we can't help it."

After a long, winding path in the musty-smelling

tunnel, a glimmer of light breaks through the darkness, framing Thor's sturdy form. Fresh air rushes in to greet us, and each of us expels an audible sigh. Our steps quicken, and before we know it, we are through the tunnel entrance to find the dragons waiting for us.

Finally! Elan's voice booms through our minds, and she dances on the spot, her front feet jumping from side to side. *You're finally back.* As soon as I step into the light, she charges up to me and nudges me with her nose. *It's so good to see you in one piece.* Towering over me, her head circles around my body as she studies every part of me.

Chuckling, I ask, "What are you doing, Elan?" Craning my neck, I watch her every move, and my head spins.

I'm checking you for any injuries.

I shove her front legs playfully. "I'm fine."

After a final once-over, she grins, showing off her vast array of threatening teeth. *All right. I believe you.* Something within the cave catches her attention, and her eyes narrow as she glares into the darkness. *Where's the dwarf?*

I place a hand on her jaw. "That's a whole other story. I'll tell you another time, but you don't need to worry. He's not going to hassle us anymore."

The goats bleat, and I turn to see them tied up to

the carriage again, ready to go. It's a good thing, since darkness is creeping into the sky, indicating we don't have time to waste.

Every one of their bleats causes my heart to ache. "I'm glad to see them in one piece. I can't imagine it would be a very nice life, living the way they do."

Tanda's red face lowers to my level on my right, her eyes set on the goats. *I didn't want to eat Thor's goats. After all, we have traveled beside them, but I was starving. We were all starving. We were still hungry afterward but not as much. I mean, look at them. They're tiny.*

After rubbing Tanngrisnir behind the ear, Thor strokes its neck. The goat connects eyes with my leader briefly and bleats at him. "They are usually designed for gods to eat, not beings as big as dragons." He shrugs. "Normally, they're a decent-sized meal, even for me, when I'm not in an eating competition." He winks at Elan.

Elan huffs. *I still say you cheated.*

Thor grabs his belt and throws his head back. His hearty laugh echoes back at us from the cave. "Is that so? Then we'll just have to have another competition soon." He lifts an eyebrow at Elan. "So, has my eating companion forgiven me?"

Pfft! Please. More like your eating champion. I could eat you under the table.

Thor grins. "Ah. You forget that I won our last competition."

Nope. Elan shakes her enormous golden scaled head. *As I said, I don't believe you did. You offloaded yours off the side of the party. I understand that would make me the winner. Next time, if you manage to eat more than me, you'll have to keep the contents in your stomach.*

"Then, when this all settles down, we'll have to do it again." Thor's second eyebrow rises in line with the first. "So, seeing you want another competition, I shall take that as a yes. You do forgive me."

Elan frowns. *Only because I heard the bargaining of your daughter was a ploy to get Alvis to take you to the blacksmiths. If you really are going to trade your daughter like that, consider me your eternal enemy. And you know I can be ferocious.* Elan snarls to emphasize the point.

Thor chuckles and places a hand on Elan's snout. "That, I know. You don't need to worry, my friend. I'm not that kind of god."

Her snarl disappears. *Good.*

My leader climbs onto his carriage and calls to the goats, sparking them into action and directing them to our exit point. After all the Valkyries are mounted, the dragons take to the sky, trailing the carriage from the air. Thor must have learned from our travels here, for this time, he doesn't use his hammer to spark thunder and lightning, creating an ominous scene and scaring the locals. Darkness closes around us, the twilight surrounding us with deep orange, red, and blue. The goats power through faster than a normal goat from Midgard.

Zildryss snuggles against my neck, and I peer over the side of Elan's golden scales at the carriage weaving its way through the trees. "I'm surprised the poor goats can go that fast after being eaten and only recently resurrecting."

That's the beauty of magic beings. They were tasty, though.

"Elan! Don't say that!" I chastise her, expecting her to be more sympathetic toward the goats.

Zildryss exits his secure spot tucked under my hair and runs up Elan's neck and grabs her horns. He must have communicated to her because, before I know it, Elan dives and flips, with Zildryss barely hanging on. At least if he falls, he has his own wings. I pull at my straps tied around my waist, making sure I'm secure.

Eventually, Elan's entertainment stops. A chilly breeze cools my face, and goose bumps rise on my arms. My long black hair whips around my face as I reach into my saddlebag and pull out my dragon-scale cloak. I wrap it around myself then thread my arms through the sleeves. Moments pass before the leather-lined scales trap in the warmth, and I snuggle into my creation. I pull my hood over my head, and Zildryss scurries down Elan's neck to snuggle within the hood's warmth against my neck.

I smile down at him. "I think you're a bit of a daredevil."

Elan peers over her shoulder. *Why do you think I'm doing all these dives and flips? He shows me how much he likes them, and that's why I do them.* Her shoulders heave. *I mean, he could be doing all the acrobatics himself —not that he could keep up with us at his size, but he does have his wings.*

Sliding my hand under a golden scale just in front of the saddle, I caress her soft skin, and smile. I'm glad that my magnificent dragon has a connection with the little newcomer.

The ground is filling with darkness, making it harder to see Thor and his carriage. At least the dragons can keep an eye on him. No home lights illuminate the way, and the sky is absent of the thunder and lightning that accompanied us to the dwarves. Then the moon begins to rise and catches on the shining metal of the carriage.

As much as I enjoy seeing the different realms, I always like to go home. Even though some realms are more beautiful than Asgard, it is still home, and that thought relaxes me.

Zildryss gives a panicked squeak, peering down

at the ground. His small body is rigid and his face taut. Elan disappears underneath me, undoubtedly transforming me with her under the veil of the cloak.

The tiny dragon wraps himself around my neck again as I study the ground.

Switching to mind speak, I ask, *What is it?*

Zildryss has seen Quash.

What? The troll's back? Isn't that okay? He was friendly with us in the end.

Yes. That was true, but this time he doesn't seem happy.

I frantically try to spot the troll in the growing darkness. I almost give up and trust Elan can deal with it when I remember learning to use her vision. I slip my hand back under her scale and focus. Within moments, the darkness fades, and I notice the trees swaying dramatically. A bald head glimmers under the moonlight, rapidly stomping toward Thor. I can't see his face, but I can certainly tell he's upset, judging by the trail of destruction he's leaving behind. I frown, trying to think of what could've happened. *Why would he be angry? Thor isn't using his thunder and lightning. Quash said that was the only reason he chased us last time.*

I don't know, but if Thor doesn't hurry up, he'll catch up to him. He's closing the distance quickly. The ground seems to rise toward me as Elan flies closer to the ground. *I'm going to let Thor know.*

Her voice goes silent in my head, and I assume she is talking to Thor. His helmet catches in the moonlight, and it tilts and spins as though he is glancing over his shoulder. The carriage increases speed as Elan lowers farther, getting closer to the carriage.

Quash swings his arms, felling trees, and bellows a boisterous roar as he trudges rapidly toward Thor.

Chapter Seventeen

My neck stiffens when another roar blocks out the rattling of the carriage wheels. "Why is he so upset? I don't understand why he would change his mind. They were getting along quite well last time."

Quash's voice reverberates through the land, rumbling up to greet us. "You killed Quash's friend." Several thunderous steps break the short silence. "Quash found his friend dead—turned to stone." *Thump, thump, thump.* The leaves on the trees rustle, creating a chorus to accompany the thrashing tune. "Quash says it was you."

The troll's face screws up in anguish as he tilts his face to the sky and screams a roar, briefly drowning out his boisterous footsteps. He accelerates toward Thor, closing the distance and seemingly oblivious to the nearby dragons.

Tanngrisnir and Tanngnjostr run faster than I

have ever seen them go. In the carriage, Thor braces his legs and has one hand holding onto the railing. He spins as far as his upper body will allow him and releases Mjollnir. The hammer wallops Quash in the chest, knocking him onto his backside, and large rocks near the troll shudder. The hammer turns and heads back to the god of thunder's outstretched hand.

"Ow!" the troll yells. "That hurt Quash. Now Quash know you killed Quash's friend." He scrambles to his feet as fast as his large form will let him and breaks into a run again. The thundering footsteps echo through the forest.

As I watch the trees, my pity grows. I can only imagine the discomfort and possibly pain they feel bending from the force of the troll's progress. His arms are thicker than Thor's waist.

Despite the destruction the troll has created, he only has angry eyes for Thor. "Quash know you killed Alvis. For this, Quash won't forgive you. Quash will avenge his friend."

A breeze blows from the troll's trail of destruction, and the scent of crushed leaves and freshly damaged woodlands washes over me. The trees continue to be pushed aside, the thin ones bending, the thicker ones almost uprooting from the force of the shove. He's causing a lot of destruction, even though he doesn't seem to have any proof. I wonder if he realizes he's destroying the home of his family. After building up a relationship with Thor earlier, he could have discussed it with him, although that is probably too intelligent for a troll.

Thor's carriage continues to dart through the trees, the goats pulling with all their strength, yet the troll still manages to close the gap between them. The length of each of the troll's steps grows seemingly longer. *Stomp, upon stomp.* The sound harasses my ears. As I gaze through Elan's vision, the knot of apprehension in my stomach grows. I have to do something. Zildryss shifts to one side of my neck when I move one side of my cloak and whip out my bow. I string an arrow from the quiver on my back then let it fly and inwardly cheer as it aims straight for the troll's outer ear and lodges in it like a strange piercing.

My inner applause washes away when the troll ignores whatever pain he feels from the imbedded arrow. Instead, he sweeps a giant hand down and wraps it around Thor, knocking his horned helmet off. It clangs on the base of the carriage as the troll hoists him. The goats are oblivious to what's happening behind them, and without the additional weight, the carriage moves faster.

I gasp. "Oh, Vanir! He's grabbed Thor."

Elan lowers to circle the troll's head, remaining invisible.

Quash's grasp tightens around Thor, pinning his arms by his side, and the troll brings Thor close to his face. The bulky god looks tiny in comparison to the size of the massive being.

"Quash, my friend!" Thor smiles, acting as though nothing is out of the ordinary. "I didn't expect to see you before we left the realm." His auburn hair hangs over his face, catching in his bushy beard. He tosses his head, attempting to move them When he's unsuccessful, he blows at the clump, shifting the loose strands slightly aside. He broadens his grin, flashing his straight white teeth as though trying to relay charm.

"Quash not your friend. Quash is angry with you." The troll shakes Thor, making Thor's head thrash from side to side.

Dismayed, Thor asks, "What do you mean? I thought we were friends, Quash, as long as I didn't do the loud thunder and lightning and scare your family."

"Quash forgave you for that if you stop doing it. That is true. But now Quash is angry with you again."

Thor pouts. "What could I possibly have done?"

The troll sits on a large boulder not far behind

him. "Quash leave you with his friend, and now Alvis is dead. Quash find him turned into stone. Now Quash is very angry."

Dread churns in the pit of my stomach, and I wonder how Thor will get out of this one. Tension tightens my shoulders and neck as Elan hovers near, ready to act if my leader can't talk his way out of this dilemma.

"I don't know what you mean." Pure innocence shines across Thor's face. "I haven't seen Alvis for a while. I just thought he left us. After all, he had completed his part of our bargain."

The troll flips Thor into the air and catches him by his legs, making him hang upside down from his fingertips. "No. You kill Quash's friend. Alvis is dead."

With his arms wide, Thor reaches for the troll, palms up. "I'm sorry to hear that, but I assure you he didn't die by my hand."

The troll shakes him, tossing the god's attempt at sympathy aside. Thor's hammer slips from his belt. He attempts to catch it but misses, and the hammer embeds itself into the ground.

"Quash doesn't believe you." The troll raises his voice. "Quash is going to kill you!" He shakes him again, and Thor sets his jaw, determination replacing his friendly expression.

As though sensing something, Elan rises much higher than Quash's head.

"Well, then. I'm sorry to hear that. I was trying to be your friend. But if you don't want to play nice." Thor reaches toward the ground, and his hammer rises and slams into his palm. His body swings from the force, though his feet remain in the troll's grasp. "Then I'm going to have to fight back." He flips up and releases the hammer onto his captor's head.

The force knocks the troll to the side, making his face hit a snapped tree trunk. Blood trickles from his eyebrow, and the hammer returns to Thor. The force makes his body swing like a pendulum. On the return swing, Thor releases the hammer again, sending it straight at the shoulder of the arm securing him. The troll's shoulder flies backward.

The troll groans, and his arm shakes, yet he still doesn't release Thor's legs. When the hammer responds to Thor's beckoning again, Quash lurches forward, shoving his angry face close to Thor's.

Ignoring the threat, Thor swings his body backward then forward and whacks the hammer onto the troll's fingers.

Quash cries out in pain and releases Thor's ankles. The god flips and falls feet first. The troll catches him with his other hand before he reaches the ground, securing Mjollnir so that he can't swing it anymore. Thor squirms within the troll's grasp, to no avail.

The troll squints at his captive as he raises him. "Quash is going to take you to his family and cook you for dinner." The large eyes flash oddly with intelligence. "Quash thinks he might skip the cooking side and just eat you raw."

"What?" Thor cries. "No!" He thrashes, panic etching his features. "I don't taste good. I can guarantee that. Wouldn't you rather eat something else?" He makes another attempt at wriggling out of the troll's grasp, but he still can't release his hands. Slowly, the troll lifts the god to his open mouth, ignoring Thor's pleas.

- Chapter Eighteen -

"Quick, Elan. We must do something." I yank out my sword and throw it at the troll's head. Maybe having a blade embedded in his flesh will grab his attention better than the arrow did. My knuckles on my left hand turn white as I grip the straps of Elan's saddle, waiting for the sword to hit. Using my magic, I direct it with my right hand to make sure its aim is true.

Quash flicks the sword away, though it slices the back of his hand. He ignores the blood running down his arm and pulls his god snack closer.

"What do we do, Elan?" I reach for my sword, calling for it. The magic wings flap my way.

Zildryss runs up Elan's invisible neck, his tiny feet feeling the way. He's traveled the path many times before, and he takes up his favorite position as he clasps her horns and peers down at the troll. It's strange to see the tiny dragon in that position with nothing underneath him. Normally, I would find it amusing, but right now, I'm too distracted.

Elan! I scream, panicking.

I'm trying to think, she snaps. *I don't know. Even I am small compared to the troll.*

My hope wavers upon hearing her self-doubt.

I search for our friends, and my heart sinks. They are a great distance ahead. They must not have heard all the commotion. Although I don't know how they could have missed it.

I'm about to suggest that Elan call them when she says, *Hold on!* She dives, twists, spins, and sweeps down at Quash, clasping his bald scalp with her talons and dragging them along his skin.

A roar fills the air as the troll throws back his head in frustration and pain, his open mouth flashing his scattered brown teeth.

"That hurt Quash!" the enormous troll yells at the sky. "Quash thought the dragon was his friend." His uses his free hand, still running with blood, to rub the top of his head as he searches the sky. "But now Quash know that you dragon are no friend. Quash can't see you, but Quash knows you're there."

He thrashes the air with his fist, narrowly missing Elan when she darts to the side. The jolting almost gives me whiplash.

Elan flaps a couple of times then dives again. She

sweeps in from the opposite side, attacking the troll from the back and dragging her talons along his neck. Her wings give a mighty push, jerking us higher with each stroke, and again narrowly misses Quash's strike. The troll's head spins in all directions as he tries to spot the invisible dragon. I don't know how he is missing Zildryss. Perhaps the lilac dragon is too small to be seen with the rapid movements.

Something catches my eye, and I glance up to see the three dragons heading our way.

Are you okay? Drogon asks gruffly.

Yes. Elan responds quickly. *I will deter him with my invisible form.* She swoops down, landing the troll with another gash to his scalp, but despite his groans of protest, Quash still doesn't let Thor go. Elan circles up. *Are you able to grab Thor when I attack next time?*

Drogon lowers closer to the troll's hand securing Thor. *Sure. I'll keep an eye out for an opening.*

Tanda and Naga circle above Quash, distracting him from Drogon and Hildr. Drogon's deep-brown color blends with the trees' trunks as Hildr aims an arrow at the back of the troll's hand. Tanda's bright-red scales catch the troll's eye, and she and Naga zigzag just out of the troll's reach as Britta and Eir cast magic spells at Quash's head.

Elan dives at Quash again, sweeping down and

dragging her talons along his scalp, adding to the existing scratches.

The cries of agony echoing through the air sends shivers down my spine, and queasiness sets in my stomach. I hate what we're doing to him. Alvis was his friend, and I understand why he would be upset about finding him turned to stone. Any of us would be upset if we found out one of our friends had died from an unnatural cause. We would probably also seek revenge.

To make matters worse, it appears as though Quash doesn't have many friends. It's a shame that Alvis didn't seem to hold Quash in the same regard. The dwarf seemed to care more about himself. Maybe he got away with it because Quash is too dimwitted to understand it.

Elan darts to the side, pulling my attention back to the fight. Even with Zildryss clearly visible, Quash doesn't seem to be bothered by him. The troll is probably too occupied with trying to fight back to realize that Zildryss is there.

In her next attack, Elan drags her talons along one of the troll's enormous ears then dodges as a massive hand covers it. Blood trickles over his palm.

The troll swings his bloodstained fist, attempting to hit his invisible attacker. At the last second, he changes the direction of his fist, aiming for the zigzagging dragons, and hits Elan. She and I flip, and my vision briefly blurs.

Hildr releases an arrow, and the whistling reaches my ears before Quash's piercing cry. The arrow's penetration into the back of the troll's hand seems to be the final straw to cause the giant to release Thor. The god of thunder falls, and Drogon catches him in his talons before he hits the ground. The brown dragon flips and heads away from the troll's reach and heads toward the Yggdrasil.

Tanda and Naga take off after Drogon.

A squeak barely captures my attention. Zildryss dives off Elan's head and glides, his little lilac wings spread wide. He somersaults in midair, missing the troll's swinging fist, and lands between the troll's shoulder blades. The tiny dragon causes the troll enough discomfort to pull the giant's attention away from Thor. Quash thrashes, jerking in different directions as he attempts to reach the menacing creature stuck between his shoulder blades. After several attempts, Quash lets out a frustrated cry and takes off after Thor.

Elan finally controls her spinning, and she hovers just out of reach of Quash, observing Zildryss's moves.

Zildryss pushes off the troll's back and lands on his enormous head, whacking his spikey tail against the side. Midstride, the troll stops. He seems frozen like a statue, yet unlike Alvis, he hasn't turned to stone. His body remains in its usual fleshy form.

A split second later, Zildryss jumps off the troll and flies above his head. Elan makes herself visible just long enough for him to find her while remaining out of the troll's reach. I study the still Quash, wondering what Zildryss has done to him. It almost seems like the lilac dragon has cast a stunning spell on the giant. It's hard to fathom that a tiny creature could perform magic to defeat a being so big.

Zildryss climbs up my cloak and circles my neck, performing his usual ritual before curling around it.

Worry seeps into my body as I gaze at the motionless figure. Our intention was never to kill the troll, only to stop him from attacking and let us leave the realm with Thor.

I run a finger over Zildryss's head and down the sides of the horns running down his spine. "What did you do? Will he be all right?"

Zildryss tilts his head far enough out to peer into my eyes. His eyes are wide as he licks his tongue from one eye to the other and shows me in my mind his distaste for the hurt we were causing Quash. Because of this, he put a stop to it by freezing him momentarily so we could get away without continuing to hurt Quash.

I rub a finger under his chin, and he nuzzles it. "Such a clever little dragon. So, he is going to be okay."

Zildryss nods and snuggles back around my neck, his smooth scales pressing against my skin and making me feel relaxed. I pull my hood over my head, securing the body heat underneath.

Elan quickly turns invisible again and accelerates, catching up to the other dragons. The branches of the Yggdrasil are not far away, and the other dragons lower, ready to enter the trunk to exit this realm. One by one, the dragons tuck their wings by their sides, their riders duck, and they dive through the hole, moving out of Svartalfheim.

Casting a final glance over my shoulder, I take in the still form of Quash. It's a shame that we couldn't stay friends with him. It would have been nice to have someone that big on our side.

Elan tucks her wings in tightly and narrowly misses the edges of the hole as she dives into the trunk. It seems to take very little time before we shoot out and into Asgard. After the excitement we just had, I'm glad to see the mundane rocky country-side once more.

Now our only hope is that this rope made by the dwarves is strong enough to hold Fenrir, or else it was all for nothing.

- Chapter Nineteen -

The sunrise peeks over the horizon, bathing Asgard in its golden light. It's a relief to see our home again, absent of the threat of Svartalfheim. Flying over the rocky landscape is a picture for the weary eyes. We fly to the palace, circle it, and land in the courtyard near the front steps. Tanda and Naga are already waiting with Britta and Eir on their backs, and Drogon lands a few moments after us. I stare at his back. Hildr sits in the saddle, and Thor is no longer draping from his talons.

My face turns numb with worry. "Where's Thor?" I had lost sight of Drogon, Hildr, and Thor after they entered the trunk of the Yggdrasil.

Hildr smirks and straightens her spikey red hair. I hope that means Thor is safe.

Loud rattling fills the courtyard, then the goat-pulled carriage charges into the open area, Thor riding on the back.

"We stopped so he could pick up his carriage. Tanngrisnir and Tanngnjostr brought it back to Asgard without realizing they left Thor behind." Hildr's auburn hair stands straight up again, catching in the sun and making it appear to be on fire.

Thor parks his goats at the front of the palace.

"Welcome back, Thor." Birger taps his heels together and pushes his shoulders back. The strap of his helmet struggles to stay on his small chin.

Gorm stands on the opposite side of the door, his solute imitating Birger's. "We trust you had a successful mission, Thor."

Thor climbs off his carriage, feeling for his hammer hanging off his belt, and I wonder how heavy it is. "Yes, thank you. We did. Although it wasn't without its hiccups. Fortunately, we had the dragons." He spots Zildryss peering out from under my hood and smiles. "All five of them and the four Valkyries accompanying them. If it weren't for them, the trip would've been much more difficult." He taps the heel of his big boots against the pavers. "Is Father home?"

Birger scratches his large nose. "Yes. We believe he's in the hall. He's been attending meetings all day."

"Thank you, Birger. Please, arrange for my goats

to be tended to and my carriage cleaned and put away. After that trip, the goats will need their rest."

"It is our pleasure, Thor." Birger yanks at the strap trying to creep above his chin. "We'll make sure they are looked after immediately."

We dismount from the dragons and follow Thor as he enters the palace doors, weaving through the marble corridors to the large hall.

Thor barges through the large etched wooden doors, ignoring the guard's protests that his father is too busy. Stepping almost directly in his footsteps, we follow him. My arrows rattle in my quiver, as though reminding me of Odin's wrath and how scared it can make me feel, but as I stare into the great god's unforgiving face, I don't need a reminder. His chin tilts up as he glowers down at a subject on all fours in the middle of the floor.

Odin catches sight of Thor and obviously disapproves of the disturbance.

Thor bows, his arms spread out and his traveling cape flailing to the side. "I apologize for interrupting, Father."

Odin stands and claps once then turns to glower at the subject. "It is an interruption, son. But I will be glad for some good news. I hope this is why you have entered my hall without waiting for my business to finish." He straightens the black eye patch covering his missing eye.

The subject whimpers, clutching at his legs and curling into a child's pose at Odin's feet.

"It has been a long and tiresome day, and good news would benefit greatly. Perhaps if I'm pleased with your news, I'll spare this person purely because of my mood."

Grabbing the sack off his back, Thor moves closer to his father's throne. "And pleasant news is what I believe we have brought. Naturally, I am not as strong as the hound, but let me assure you that this is not what it seems." He dips his hand into the bag and retrieves the rope, which looks thin and frail. "I've been informed it is stronger than any of the chains we have ever produced on Asgard."

Odin scowls, and I hold my breath as Thor hands the part of the rope to him.

With his face set in a scowl, Odin feels it between his fingers. "Are you sure this is strong, son?" He runs his fingers along the fabric again, and his eyes fill with confusion. "It feels flimsy. Have you tried it?"

"I have been assured by the dwarves that this is stronger than any chains we have. It appears weak, but it's made with rare ingredients with magic woven into its strands. It will be impossible to break."

"Hmm." Odin paces the room, wrapping the rope around his arm, and circles to the front of the subject still sprawled on the floor. "You," he says harshly.

Still facing to the floor, the subject glances through his eyelashes at the god, terror plastered all over his face. "Yes, great Odin." His voice is barely audible.

Odin flicks a hand at him. "Call this your lucky day. You're dismissed… this time."

The man's mouth drops open before he silently scrambles to his feet and sidesteps Thor on his way past. He tilts his head in a final gesture of respect. "Thank you, great Odin."

Without giving the man a second glance, Odin continues to pace, his fingers still working the threads. "There's only one way to find out. Isn't there? Call the other gods to meet us at the usual field where Fenrir likes to show off his strength. We'll need some backup just in case. Make sure Tyr brings Fenrir. He seems to have a connection with that dreaded hound."

Thor inclines his head. "First, I would like to make it clear that this mission wouldn't have been a success without the help of these four Valkyries and their dragons. They got me out of many… let's just say sticky situations."

Odin's one-eyed gaze travels across the Valkyries and halts on me. He shows no familiarity from the days when I helped him hide his meltdown. Instead, his gaze remains cold and unfamiliar, although at least it doesn't carry the usual spite or anger it has often held of late.

Still, trying to win back his favor after my mishap of releasing Loki, I bow my head slightly, showing him my appreciation. "Thank you, great Odin. I am pleased to be of service for securing Asgard's future."

The four of us wait in a small line to be dismissed.

I feel Odin's eye pass over each of us as he saunters past. "Well? What are you waiting for?" His feet quicken, his long burgundy cape flowing behind him as he exits the hall.

We scurry after Odin, our boots scuffing on the marble floor, then we weave through the corridors and out the door past Birger and Gorm. Like loyal friends, our dragons wait for us expectantly in the courtyard.

Thank you for waiting, but all of you dragons are free to go. I decide to use my mind speak, not wanting to test Odin's patience any further. *Thank you for all your hard work. I'll catch up with you soon.*

Elan tilts her head to the side. *And where are you going?*

We're trying out the rope on Fenrir. Odin's not wasting any time, I say.

Are you sure you don't want us to come? Her brow furrows pushing the golden scales together. *It sounds dangerous.*

I shrug. *We should be fine. But if you really want to come, maybe you should hang around the outskirts of the field. It's up to you. If you want to be our companions, tag along.*

Disbelieving, she gazes at the other dragons as though seeking their opinion. *Of course we want to be your companions,* she snaps. *And we care about you, so that is why we need to keep an eye on you.*

Hearing her displeasure, I say, *Of course you care for us. I know that. It's not what I'm saying.* I glance at Odin, who's holding his head high and his shoulders stiff. *If you decide to stay, I think it's best if you keep out of Odin's sight for now. Hopefully this rope is as strong as they claim. If not, we'll likely need your help.*

- Chapter Twenty -

Britta, Eir, Hildr, and I stand in the training area, waiting for Thor to gather the rest of the gods and for the arrival of Tyr and Fenrir.

"I'm nervous," Eir admits, breaking the silence. When none of us respond, she adds, "I feel bad that we're going to restrain Fenrir."

I've been mulling that feeling over. Fenrir was such an adorable pup. It's upsetting to think that we have to treat him this badly. I open my mouth to agree with Eir, but I'm interrupted.

"We can only hope it works." Hildr's usual gruff tone grates like sandpaper, and my sadness deepens as I wish there were a way to reason with Fenrir.

Britta pulls at the hem of her leather uniform top. "If it doesn't work, it could turn out to be a mess."

Scanning the horizon, I search unsuccessfully for the dragons. "I told Elan that the dragons could leave, but she insisted that they would be staying just in case. They should be close. Because I never know what is going through Odin's head these days, I asked for them to stay out of sight."

Britta looks up from studying the edges of her uniform, her brow lined with worry. "Hopefully we won't need them."

Something brown catches the corner of my eye. I turn to find Fenrir padding beside Tyr. Fenrir makes the god of war look puny. It's almost comical. To think that he adopted the dog when he was only a puppy—an enormous puppy yet still a puppy. The difference from that puppy's face to the screwed-up teenage face of the hound is unnerving. As if to prove a point, when Fenrir's eyes land on me, his snout retracts some more, exposing the length of his giant fangs. I'm not sure why he dislikes me so much these days. I did recapture his father, but it's Odin's ruling that has him imprisoned. I wouldn't think the hound would be worried about being tied up by this restraint. He has managed to break through every other chain around his neck.

It breaks my heart to see Tyr's face set with resignation. The deep sadness turns the corners of his eyes down. Strands of dark hair fall over the god of war's eyes, and he doesn't bother to move them. I wonder if he believes that this is the rope that will be successful in restraining Fenrir.

They approach, taking their time, and when they draw near, Fenrir snarls at me. His brown fur is matted and unkempt, like a teenage boy's hair. "Why don't you come here, little Valkyrie? Let me teach you a lesson about entrapping my father." He gives a low guttural growl, exposing more of his teeth.

I back away and snap, "If your father had behaved, I wouldn't have had to recapture him." Seeing the hound's anger rising, I realize that probably wasn't the best thing to say. I lighten my tone. "If he proves himself, I'm sure the gods will let him go again."

Snarling, Fenrir tosses his head to the side. "Huh. How little you know about the gods."

Tyr moves between Fenrir and me and strokes the hound, his fingers snagging between the fibers. "Calm down, Fenrir. She's only doing her job. If you want to burn off your aggression, take it out on Odin. It's his ruling." The touch of the god of war's hand seems to calm the hound, especially when it travels over Fenrir's crown.

Fenrir tilts his head toward Tyr and nuzzles into his side. Tyr wraps his arms around the enormous head, compassion written all over his face. The bond between them is evident, despite Fenrir's recent grumpiness.

Fenrir grins at Tyr. The expression is similar to a

snarl, except his eyes are soft, not sharp and aggressive. "I can't wait to prove how stupid their little restraint will be." He turns to us, and the softness in his eyes is replaced instantly with a harsh, piercing expression. Fenrir growls. "I'm sure your trip was a waste of time, and I'm going to prove it."

Tyr runs a calloused hand down Fenrir's brown-furred cheek then over his shoulder. "Okay, Fenrir. Save your energy for the restraint. You can take out all your aggression against that."

A low growl rattles the bottom of the hound's throat. "Oh, I intend to. Watch it snap like the fragile thing it is."

Tyr directs the hound farther away from us, and Fenrir plonks his backside on the ground, watching the gods descend into the training area. I don't need to see the hound's face to know his teeth are showing. The snarl only softens when Tyr hooks a muscular arm around his front leg. I don't know whether it's intentional or the god is nervous, but in the arm securing the hound, the muscles flex as though he's bracing the leg and trying to restrain him from attacking the gods.

"Aww."

I glance at Britta to find admiration written all over her face.

"You can't seriously be ogling the gods," I say.

She shakes her head. "No. Just Balder. I can't get over the shine of his skin and how light his blond hair is."

Clenching my teeth, I reply, "Get ahold of yourself. Now's not the time. You need to be focused in case things go wrong."

Her shoulders slump. "I know. You're right. But I'll definitely be looking later." She grins.

Odin carries the restraint looped around his arm, his fingers still fiddling with the thin fabric. He portrays confidence, but when he comes closer, I swear uncertainty is dancing in his eyes. He pulls at the rope as though trying to restore faith in the magic held within the flimsy material.

Fenrir stands tall. "What's that hanging over Odin's arm?"

I push aside my fear of the hound, letting my pity do the talking. "That's the restraint. That's what you have to tackle this time."

The hound narrows his eyes on me and growls. "Who asked you to speak?"

Instantly I regret that I let my sympathy rule me for a moment. I swallow, willing away the threat from the hound's gaze. I've certainly made an enemy out of this one. It's still hard to believe that this threatening creature used to be the cutest and most affectionate puppy. But now, no matter what anyone says, he seems to take offense. It's not our fault his father betrayed Asgard.

When the gods are close enough to hear, Fenrir jeers, "What do you expect to do with that?"

I cringe at his arrogance. He has no idea this rope is deceptive.

Odin chuckles, holding the rope high to show it off. "This is your restraint."

A garbled sound comes from Fenrir, and it takes me a moment to realize he's chuckling. "When the Valkyrie informed me, I thought she was joking. That is nothing but a sheer piece of fabric. It can't be stronger than a spiderweb."

Odin raises an eyebrow over his seeing eye, the challenge in his gaze evident. "Then you'll have no qualms about us wrapping it around your neck. Surely you'll be able to break a flimsy piece of fabric."

When the gods near, the enormous hound stands on all fours, towering over them. He exposes more of his teeth with each of their steps in his direction. Odin looks so small against his mighty form, yet he approaches with his son, surrounded by the gods, his broad chest puffed out. The great leader holds the restraint up close to Fenrir and allows the hound to sniff it.

Fenrir backs away, distrust etched on his furry

face. "It smells of trickery." He loudly exhales from his nose as though ridding his snout of its scent before he pads closer and takes a long final sniff before backing away again, snarling. "Yes. It certainly does."

Odin's aging face somehow expresses pure innocence. "But you said it's only thin fabric. You should be able to break through a fabric this thin much quicker than any of the other restraints. Shouldn't you? After all, they were heavy chains, and remember what you did to them. You proved to us that you are mighty. Wouldn't you like to prove that again?"

I grasp a handful of my uniform, full of tension.

Fenrir isn't one to be tricked easily, and the astuteness washing over his face proves he isn't convinced. He sits back on his haunches next to Tyr and stares at the restraint. "Yes, the others were broad and strong. It was obvious that they were strong, and I proved that I could smash through them." He lifts his chin, showing his pride, yet a wariness flashes over the hound's face. "So why do I have to prove myself over this? It won't look spectacular if I break through a thin piece of fabric. It will undo all of my hard work of proving my strength."

Odin appears thoughtful. "I don't know what you think you can lose." The god fiddles with the fabric, running his fingers along the fibers, accentuating its softness. "As you said, it's only a thin piece of fabric. We have seen how you broke through the big thick chains. We will remember that. Your breaking this won't disintegrate the value of the strength."

Fenrir narrows his eyes, the look of intelligence getting sharper. "I still smell trickery. And I won't put myself through it without some sort of sacrifice on your end." He lifts his chin showing his defiance. "The gods must sacrifice something."

Odin chuckles and grins. "I'm sure we could come to an arrangement. What do you have in mind?"

The hound cocks an eyebrow and tilts his head to one side. "If I can break through this, then you lose nothing. Isn't that right?"

Odin's grin broadens as though he's plastering on every bit of friendliness he can muster. "Of course. So, what is it that you request?" he asks again.

Fenrir straightens his shoulders, pushing on his front legs, and he gazes down at the gods, his brown eyes sharp and untrusting. "One of you must put your arm in my mouth. If you don't believe this is trickery, then you will have no problem doing this. If I can break free from this restraint, then the arm is unharmed. If not, then the volunteer will lose an arm."

Chapter Twenty-One

Color seeps from the gods' faces, and a ripple of tension goes through the group.

"What's wrong?" Fenrir asks. "You said this is just a flimsy thing. If it is, then there is no threat to you."

Odin clears his throat. "Of course. You are correct." He opens his arms, gesturing broadly. "One of us should definitely do as you ask as proof of our sincerity." He glances at the gods around him, including his sons. Each of them turns paler by the second, darting their eyes and retreating slightly.

Balder moves in front of the hound. "I'll do it."

Fenrir spits. "Not a chance. Don't you think I know about the oath everything swore to your mother? I can't harm you, rendering no risk to the gods."

All eyes fall to Tyr, who's still standing next to the

hound. He releases a long sigh, the severity of his risk weighing heavily on his shoulders, and steps forward. "I'll do it. I was the one to raise him, so I should show him the most confidence and trust."

A strange look passes through Fenrir's eyes as Tyr offers him his arm, and he clamps his teeth around it.

Odin claps once. "Right. That's settled, then." He doesn't seem to spare a thought for Tyr.

The gods set to work, grabbing the rope from Odin and wrapping it once around Fenrir's neck. It knots easily, securing firmly, and they tie the other end around a large boulder not far away.

With each movement, the god of war's face turns paler.

Odin strokes his abdomen slowly and rocks on his feet. "Okay, Fenrir. The restraint is secure. Now show us how tough you are."

Within moments, the hound is pulling, twisting, and yanking at the restraint. The first effort is half-hearted, but the intensity grows with each failed attempt. The hound's teeth scrape against Tyr's arm with each movement, and the muscles in the god of war's jaw ripple with each scrape. Tyr attempts to move with the hound's movements, yet with all the thrashing, it's not surprising that he still gets hurt. Thin lines of blood trickle down Tyr's arm, but the hound continues.

Several times Fenrir tries without success, the frustration growing with each attempt. Usually, Fenrir would have escaped by now. Yet he isn't having any luck against this thin piece of fabric.

Out of breath, Fenrir sits on his haunches, panting. His large brown eyes focus on Tyr. "It's not looking so good for you, is it?"

Tyr's jaw clenches, and sweat pools on his brow. His dark hair sticks to his skin. His eyes are compassionate yet pleading. "You just need to try again, Fenrir. You have proven us wrong with every other restraint. Surely you can prove us wrong with this one."

Once the hound regains some of his breath, he stands and attempts again. His movements are solid, yet he tries not to hurt Tyr. Tyr's teeth clench, his eyes saddening further with each failed attempt.

Making matters worse, the gods begin to laugh at the beast's attempts. Horror seizes me, and I back away, realizing what will soon happen. Although I want the restraint to work, I hoped that Fenrir's love for Tyr would keep him from removing the god's arm. It doesn't appear that love will win at this stage.

The gods' laughing doesn't help, and it grows with each failed attempt, making Fenrir more irritated. Fenrir's pride is getting hurt, and he will want punishment.

A small voice rises against the laughter. "Stop it, gods!" A rare frown creases Eir's peaceful face, and she moves closer to the jeering mob. "Can't you see your taunting is making things worse?"

The gods pause and glance at Odin as though looking for instruction. The leader tilts his head back and blows a raspberry. The laughter ignites again.

Eir's shoulders slump. "This isn't good. I mean, it's good that it's successful in restraining Fenrir, but it's not good for Tyr. Look at his face." She points at the god of war and the hopeless realization evident on his face.

Yet the gods continue their mocking, allowing it to grow with each of Fenrir's failed attempts.

His struggle seems to continue for hours, the uncomfortable feeling it gives me dragging out the time. Panting, Fenrir drops to his haunches. Hesitantly, he says to the god who raised him, "You know what this means, don't you?"

Sadness, understanding, and surrender flash across Tyr's face. He nods once, gazing deep into the Fenrir's brown eyes. Without wasting a second, the hound chomps Tyr's arm, severing it before spitting it out on the other side.

To stop my cry, I slap a hand over my mouth.

Britta turns away quickly then, with a distorted

face, peers back at Tyr. "Oh, that's horrible! Tyr raised him from a pup. You'd think he'd show some kind of reservation over hurting him."

Hildr's freckled face screws up in disgust. "Even I admit that's terrible. But Tyr knew the risks, and he knows that the hound needs to be restrained. He's turned into a monster."

Pulling a bandage out of her bag, Eir attempts to stop the bleeding. "Let's get you to Anita. I don't know if she can reattach limbs, but it's worth a try."

Balder hooks his shoulder under Tyr's remaining arm. "I'll take him."

Eir's cheeks turn pink under the god of light's gaze. "Oh. All right." She releases Tyr into Balder's care and watches him as he scoops up the dismembered arm from the ground.

Fenrir's sad brown eyes follow his keeper's retreat before turning to ice as he faces Asgard's great ruler. "I'll get you, Odin. This's your fault. I'll destroy you." He snaps at the god, pulling against his restraint.

The other gods act quickly, grabbing a large stick and shoving it into the hound's open mouth to jam it open.

Dribble runs down each side of the ravenous beast's mouth as he thrashes, his eyes wild. Even with his mouth lodged wide open, the hound still calls threats to Odin. "I will get you. This, I guarantee."

Odin moves directly in front of the hound, crossing his arms and chuckling. "You wish, Fenrir. You wish. Enjoy your life of being harnessed to the rock." He nods at the large boulder, his shoulder-length gray hair glistening in the sun, before walking away. "I think it's time for celebration!" he yells. "Make sure you inform the einherjar. The warriors need to be included. There's going to be a huge party on Asgard tonight."

Fenrir pulls at his restraints, attempting to snap at Odin despite his mouth being held open. He struggles, tossing his head and flicking drool across the remaining gods. He snarls at each god that approaches him.

With heavy hearts, we Valkyries make our way to where the dragons lie in wait then head up the hill, leaving the training area behind. None of us looks back at the thrashing hound.

Britta falls in step beside me. "What happened today seems cruel, and it makes me sad. Still, I'm glad that one of Loki's monster children is sorted, at least for now."

I move slowly next to her, rubbing my long black

sleeve. "I agree. Although I dread to think of what may be next." Letting my mind process the information, I take a few more steps before continuing. "I think this one is harsher because we know Fenrir was once a cute pup."

Chapter Twenty-Two

Cheers and laughter fill the hall of Valhalla, drowning out the blaring music and spilling outside, where more gods of Asgard and einherjar gather in groups under the Yggdrasil, close to Heidrun's mead.

The dragons have returned briefly to the waste-lands to spend time with their families before they're needed for another mission. Although I'm happy that Fenrir will no longer be a problem, I can't help thinking that this is the calm before the storm. Something is causing my stomach to stir, and despite the merriment surrounding me, I'm finding it hard to join in. I wish Elan were here. She would help me get past this uneasiness.

I spot a trickle of mead falling into the large pot and head straight to the bottom of the Yggdrasil. The lemon-colored silk of my dress rubs against my legs, and my movements feel awkward. I wish I could have worn my uniform. I would feel much more at ease. Except Thor insisted that this is a night of merriment, and even I wasn't to wear my uniform.

I stand near the bowl and pull on the single strap at my shoulder. The light lemon fabric is tight around my bodice and flows to the ground from my hips. It's not a color I would've chosen in the past, but something about it reminds me of Elan, which warms my heart. I cross my ankles and lean against the trunk of the world tree. I'm glad I opted for yellow flats studded with diamonds instead of heels. On top of the awkward dress, I would also have tripped over everything.

A group of einherjar clink their pewter cups together and lift them in a toast. They look so joyous, yet the celebration of the gods and warriors won't rub off on me. I keep seeing images of Tyr losing his arm and the angry beast, who was once a beautiful puppy, literally drooling at the mouth for revenge. I don't know how everyone here can just shove that aside.

I grab a pewter pint mug from the table nearby and dip it into the large pot of mead. "Perhaps this will help," I mutter before taking a sip. The liquid trickles down my throat, making my belly warm and arms tingle.

I catch sight of another dribble entering the pot, and I gaze up toward Heidrun's bleating.

"Hello, girl. I think you'll be better company for me tonight. I hope you don't mind."

She lowers her head, and I scratch her behind her ears. Bleats of enjoyment are my thanks.

"It's good to be around you too," I say then take another sip from my cup. I'm not sure Heidrun understands me, but I don't mind. Animals have always brought me comfort. Their presence doesn't bring trickery or malice. The connection is simple and straightforward.

Heidrun climbs the branches and chews the leaves above me. Every few bites, she sticks her brown-and-white head through the leaves and bleats, her tongue working the latest mouthful. I take another sip of mead and watch her. I've found a new respect for goats since our last mission, especially the goats of Asgard. As for Thor's goats, Tanngrisnir and Tanngnjostr, they have my utmost admiration. What they have to go through and how they manage is beyond me.

I twirl the few long black strands of hair falling out of my half bun and take another sip of mead as I marvel over Heidrun.

"I didn't recognize you." Britta's voice cuts through my thoughts.

I release my strands of hair, and my jaw drops. Britta's wearing a long red dress that hugs her every curve, and her brown hair is scooped into a tight bun. Only a few wispy strands frame her pale face.

"Wow!" I look her up and down. "You're one to talk. I'm sure you're catching the eyes of the warriors."

She giggles, the sound girly for the battle maiden. "I think I'm trying to catch a god's attention, not a warrior's." Her gaze travels to a group surrounding Balder.

The god of light's clear skin has its usual glow, literally shining, and his blond hair falls around his face. Gold thread embroiders the edges of his tunic, and a gold belt circles his waist. I have to admit he does look nice. However, I keep my thoughts to myself.

"I'd have to agree." Hildr stands on her other side, and not seeing her sword by her side is strange enough, let alone the figure-hugging dress she's wearing. I have to blink twice to register that this is my tough friend wearing a low-cut V-neck beige dress edged in gold. The color suits her short auburn hair and her light scattering of freckles.

I shake my head, trying to clear away the dress's effects. "What do you mean?"

"I'm talking about Balder, of course. He's quite a

catch." Even though she's almost yelling to be heard over the music, Hildr's voice sounds dreamy.

I roll my eyes, happy to be distracted by Eir approaching in her pale-blue gown. A long braid of light-brown hair runs down her back. It's laced with flowers, reminding me of the time we spent in Alfheim with the elves. She must be missing the elf she met there, her love interest.

She glances over at Balder and shrugs. "He's a god. Although he's a nice god, and he's all for peace. He gets extra points for that, but I have somebody else in mind."

"Maybe you can go visit after this," I suggest. "Now that Fenrir is restrained, we shouldn't have any immediate dramas. You should take the time to visit him."

She smiles sweetly, light filling her eyes. "I might just do that. I got a message from him before I came out tonight. Through Ratatoskr, of course." She rolls her eyes. "It's a very delicate process sending and receiving an insult from a peace-loving person. I wish there were a better way."

"Then we have to make a better way. Nothing's better than seeing each other face to face." I elbow her softly. "So, does he want you to visit?"

"He says he does." She frowns. "I think, in a backward way through insults."

"Well, then. There's your answer." I hook my arm through hers.

"Yes. Naga is keen to get back to the peaceful realm, too, after spending time in such a harsh one." She looks away with a wistful expression. "He told me so just before he left for the wastelands."

A loud group of gods and warriors surround Balder, capturing our attention again. Each one takes a turn lining up their weapon and firing it directly at him.

Hildr sighs. "Here we go again."

Britta clasps her hands in front of her. "I think it's adorable."

"To a point," Hildr says. "Although I wish I had that gift. It would be nice not to have to worry about anything hurting you."

Most of the cheer and chatter dies down as several warriors continue to aim their bows at Balder. A combined twang sounds as all the arrows are released together. When they reach only half an inch away from the god, they simply drop to the ground in a large pile at his feet. Everyone laughs, including Balder. Once again, he remains unharmed, protected by the oath that all things not harm him, as his mother demanded.

A man in a wheelchair, looking dejected, catches my eye. He sits apart from Balder's group.

"Who's that?" I ask.

Hildr follows my gaze. "Oh. That's Hodr, Balder's brother. Odin and Frigg's other son."

I study the man for a while. "He looks sad."

She fiddles with the plunging neckline of her dress. "Yeah. He can't join in with the fun because he's blind."

"How do you know?" I clasp her fidgeting hand.

She smiles, knowing I was stopping her nervous fiddling. "Don't ask. I know things sometimes." She shrugs. "I'd say he is sad. It would be kind of depressing hearing all the merriment and not seeing it and joining in. It's not like these warriors hold intelligent conversations."

I cross my arms. "Okay. Then who's the elderly woman next to him, whispering in his ear?" I raise an eyebrow. "Seeing how you think you know things."

She frowns, and the light spray of freckles on her forehead pushes together. After studying the female, she shakes her head. "I don't know." She takes another look. "I've never seen her before."

"What's she doing with that spear? She's placing it in Hodr's hand and is directing him toward Balder."

Eir plays with the end of her braid. "Aw. That's sweet... I mean, in a weird way."

Britta looks amused. "Whoever she is, she's

helping Hodr join in the fun. As weird as it is that everyone is trying to hurt him."

Watching the woman set up the spear makes me feel strange, but I decide it's because the warriors wanting to throw potentially deadly items at the invincible god is disconcerting. Or maybe it's the size of the weapon being loaded into Hodr's hands. "It is a bit sick."

"Yeah," Britta says, the shine in her eyes dimming.

The woman's veil of gray hair droops over her face as she holds the spear steady in Hodr's hand and whispers in his ear. He nods and smiles, and she guides his arm, then he releases the spear. The aim is true. The spear flies directly at Balder's chest.

Balder spots the spear coming from Hodr and opens his arms wide. Seeing his blind brother participating in the shenanigans makes his face glow brighter. His smile broadens, and the crowd cheers until the spear lands directly in Balder's heart.

Chapter Twenty-Three

"Ah… what?" Britta's voice pierces the silence, seemingly sparking the surrounding crowd into action.

Several gods and warriors run to Balder's aid.

"What happened? He's invincible," she continues.

Thor cradles Balder in his arms, his face distraught. The light god remains unmoving. The ugly spear juts to the sky.

My face is numb, and my feet refuse to move. "Something has gone wrong."

Wailing cuts the air, a high-pitched keening that will haunt me. The spectators gather around the prone god, blocking our view of the disaster.

I search the area for the woman, but she has disappeared. *Strange.* It's all peculiar. Everything in the universe has sworn an oath to Frigg that they won't hurt her son. It makes me wonder what the woman gave Hodr to aim at Balder. I didn't think anything could break that promise.

The crowd keens Balder's name in unfaltering grief. Each cry breaks my heart a little more. Thor must be beside himself. His brother has been killed by another brother.

Something shifts in the center of the crowd, and my heart flutters with hope. But when the group separates, all that hope is smashed. With Balder gathered in his arms, Thor walks to the palace. The wailing of the crowd follows him.

Eir wipes a tear from under her eye and rubs it on her gown. The dampness leaves a dark patch on her pale-blue dress. "I wish we could heal him, but I don't know anyone who can bring a being back from the dead." She sniffles. "We have all these powers and some healing ability, yet there is so much we still cannot do."

"Why can't you do it?" I recoil at Britta's aggressive tone before realizing it's just her way of dealing with the grief. "Why can't you heal him?"

I have no answer. I just shake my head and hurry to catch up with Thor. Eir falls in beside me. We follow him into the palace, leaving the grieving crowd behind. Thor carries Balder into one of the spare palace rooms and lays him on the bed, flicking the draping curtains over the box frame above the bed.

Thor yanks the spear out of his brother's heart and lays it on the ground then sits on the edge of the bed, placing his hand over the hole in his brother's chest.

Eir sits on the bed near Balder's head, pulls Thor's hand aside gently, and replaces it with hers. She pumps as much healing magic into him as she can muster. "Maybe he's not dead." The optimism in her voice is almost as heartbreaking as Balder's death.

I don't believe it will work, but I take my place next to her on the bed and follow her lead. It wouldn't hurt to at least try.

Thor rises from the bedside and stands back, letting us work. He paces the floor and wrings his hands, his brow furrowed with worry. As if this isn't nerve-wracking enough, he mutters continuously, "This can't be. This can't be. This can't be." He shakes his head as if to expel the horrible nightmare. "Mother will die distraught."

Hearing this doesn't aid my helplessness, but it does power me with more ferocity to try to heal him.

Several minutes pass without any improvement. Not a thing changes about Balder's appearance, and the gaping hole remains in his chest. We pump more healing magic into him only to pull away unrewarded, exhausted, and cold.

I hold my cheek above his mouth, hoping for some warm breath to caress it and search for a rise of his ribs, but I come up short. I check his carotid artery. "There's no pulse." I give Eir an earnest look. "We cannot raise him from the dead."

Eir's brown eyes are a swamp of worry. "There must be something we can do."

Thor finally takes a seat, his blue eyes glistening with tears, and he buries his head in his hands.

A high-pitched wail streams through the doorway, and a beautiful woman with blond hair flowing down her back glides into the room, her face distorted in anguish. Eir and I shift from the bed, and she sits by Balder's side, clutching his hand. Neverending rivers of tears trickle down her face. Puffy redness surrounds her eyes, which fix on the prone god before her. "No. No. No," she cries over and over again. "Everything in the universe swore an oath not to harm you. Everything promised." She struggles to speak past her tears and swallows. "Only one weak little vine didn't. It was so tiny and flimsy that I didn't make it promise."

This must be Balder's mother, Frigg.

His eyes bleary, yet alert, Thor looks at his stepmother. "And what was that?"

"Mistletoe," she whispers hoarsely, turning her tear-stained face toward my leader. "It was so tiny that it wouldn't have been able to harm anything."

Thor stands and scoops up the spear to study its wood. He holds it closer for Frigg to see. "Well, it's not scrawny now. It's strong enough to be carved into a spear, albeit a small one. It's still big enough to pierce a heart."

Wails echo as the goddess bows over her son's body, sobs rocking her torso. "How could I have missed it?" Her muffled cry will haunt my nightmares. "Why did I miss even the tiny little thing?" More sobs rain out, painting the room thick with grief. "I should have made everything swear. Everything!"

Thor wipes his eyes with his sleeve then places a hand on Frigg's back. "Did anyone know about the mistletoe?"

She pushes off the bed and shakes her head. "No." Then her shoulders stiffen. "Actually, only the other day, I whispered the knowledge to a sweet old lady."

My stomach whirls. "An old lady helped Hodr direct the spear." My soft voice sounds foreign. I don't want to bring more bad news to the goddess.

Her blank stare lands on me, and the additional guilt seems to hit her like a chariot. "Oh."

I swallow. I'm not prepared for the tears that stream down her face, stripping the gorgeous goddess of all beauty.

Somehow she manages to push out past her shaking lips, "It's my fault." Her voice breaks. "It's my fault he's dead." The tears stream off her chin and pool on the blankets.

Thor draws away to the corner, his eyes distant.

Hearing Frigg's grief is unsettling me to my bones. Not knowing what to do, I place a hand on my leader's forearm. "I'm sorry, Thor. I wish there were something we could do, but we aren't necro-mancers. We cannot raise the dead."

Suddenly, Thor's eyes sharpen, and the hope I see almost knocks me to the floor. "There may be one thing we can do, Mother. It's a long shot, but it's worth a try." I can tell he's trying to keep the hope out of his voice.

She looks up, her eyes full of light despite Thor's attempts to keep his hope at bay. "What's that?"

"Balder didn't die an honorable death, warranting him a spot in Valhalla. This means he would have gone to Helheim."

Her lips quiver at what seems like an insult rather than hope.

Thor avoids her gaze and scratches the toe of his boot on the floor. "This time, it could work in our favor. Perhaps because he has such a good nature and doesn't deserve to be punished, we can reason with Hel. Maybe she will see our reasoning and release him back to the world of the living." Thor fidgets some more. "As I said, it's a long shot. Rumors say she has been causing grief over her father being captured."

Grasping Thor with one hand and Balder with the other, Frigg says, "Please, do this. Please. *Please*, help bring him back."

Thor takes a deep breath then meets my eyes. "I will go, Mother. But I need to take my trusted Valkyrie and her friends with me. Helheim is a dangerous place."

THE END

SHROUDED: book 5 in Thor's Dragon Rider series can be found here: https://books2read.com/u/mvqwOl

IF YOU ENJOYED RELINQUISHED, please take a few minutes and leave a review on Amazon. Thank you. Reviews help authors.

Get updates & notifications of giveaways

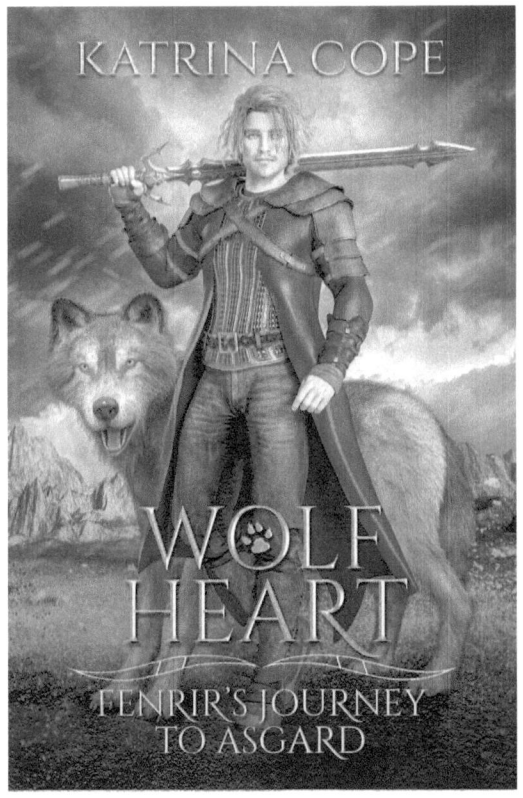

Would you like a FREE ebook?

Click here to get started: FREE copy of Wolf Heart: Fenrir's Journey to Asgard or go to https://BookHip.com/KQGGZF

Through this link you can sign up for my newsletter and

receive a FREE copy of Wolf Heart plus updates about my fantasy books, sales and notification of giveaways.

ACKNOWLEDGMENTS

Thank you to all of the creators of literature and websites who have spent time writing about Norse Mythology. Even though at times there has been contradicting information, it has been an interesting study. After all, of course a goat produces mead, and a dragon gnaws at the roots of the Yggdrasil, unhindered, threatening the existence of the nine realms attached to the world tree. Plus, there are many other "believable" tales told.

Norse mythology is such an impressive set of tales that I have incorporated some and invented others to create Kara and Elan's story.

I am touched by the enormous amount of support I have received from my immediate family. My husband has been a helpful first reader and, at times, been an excellent motivator, with hints of ideas to help me through the blanks. The support from my three sons has also been overwhelming. They have spent years putting up with my head in the clouds, thinking about the next plot twist or story, along with many hours spent working on my books and keeping in touch with my readers.

A big thank you to my extended family, who support me being a book enthusiast.

A huge thank you to my editor, Susie Driver, her editing and writing tips, and my proofreader, Virge B., for picking up the things we missed.

Thank you to all of my readers who have loved my work, and continue to read my stories.

BOOKS BY KATRINA COPE

Pre-Teen Books

The Sanctum Series

JAYDEN'S CYBERMOUNTAIN

SCARLET'S ESCAPE

TAYLOR'S PLIGHT

ERIC & THE BLACK AXES

ADRIANNA'S SURGE

~~~~~

Young Adult Urban Fantasy

Afterlife Series

FLEDGLING

THE TAKING

ANGELIC RETRIBUTION

DIVIDED PATHS

TRUTH HUNTER

Afterlife Novelette

THE GATEKEEPER

~~~~~

Young Adult Urban Paranormal Fantasy

Supernatural Evolvement Series

(Associated with the Afterlife Series)

WITCH'S LEGACY (Prequel)

AALIYAH

~~~~~

Young Adult Norse Mythology Fantasy

Valkyrie Academy Dragon Alliance

MARKED (Prequel)

CHOSEN

VANISHED

SCORNED

INFLICTED

EMPOWERED

AMBUSHED

WARNED

ABDUCTED

BESIEGED

DECEIVED

Thor's Dragon Rider

SAFEGUARD

PURSUIT

ENTRAPMENT

HOODWINKED

RELINQUISHED

SHROUDED

More to come

ABOUT THE AUTHOR

Katrina is a best-selling author of young adult fantasy and middle grade/tween novels. Her novels incorporate action, heart and an intriguing plot.

She resides in Queensland, Australia. Her three teenage boys and husband for over twenty years treat her like a princess. Unfortunately though, this princess still has to do domestic chores.

From a very young age, she has been a very creative person and has spent many years travelling the world and observing many different personalities and cultures. Her favourite personalities have been the strange ones, yet the ones under the radar also hold a place in her heart.

Katrina's online home is at www. katrinacopebooks.com
    You can connect with Katrina on:
    Facebook Group

facebook.com / Author.Katrina.Cope

twitter.com / Katrina_R_Cope

instagram.com / katrina_cope_author

pinterest.com / katrinacope56

bookbub.com / profile / katrina-cope